The Crisis Denied

The Crisis Denied

Gerald Naber

To order additional copies of this book, contact:
Xlibris
1-888-795-4274
www.Xlibris.com
Orders@Xlibris.com
784565

Contents

Chapter 1

Max

This story begins during the year 2050 near Kandahar, Afghanistan. A Special Forces unit was in the process of mopping up a significant enemy engagement. Tracy, an American diplomat, escorted by a young officer, arrived at the scene of the conflict and was aghast at the carnage that had taken place. They were dispatched there to write a report on the battle. Immediately they noticed that no prisoners were taken and nine of the enemy may have been executed! Each of these nine enemies had a 45-caliber slug in their head. Only Master Sargent Max, the man in charge of the unit, carried a 45-caliber handgun!

The Army General in the Kandahar area at the time of this battle was "Ranger". Out of respect, he was addressed as "Ranger", rather than his name, because of his remarkable thirty-year career in the US Army Rangers. He was made General during the plague.

Max was frequently the tool Ranger used to take on difficult situations. He needed Max and many times overlooked what might have happened in the fog of war. Max was known to accomplish the impossible. It was also said, that his men would follow him through the gates of Hell! Every one in his unit was treated with the highest respect.

After Tracy turned in the report on their findings of the battle to Ranger, it was soon misplaced. Ranger noticed shock on Tracy and the young officer's face and decided to handle this situation immediately. He quickly redeployed the young officer to Iraq and had Tracy returned to her present assignment in South America. In addition, Max was spirited out of Afghanistan to the United States.

Max requested, at this time, to finish out his career at Offutt Air Force Base, near Omaha, Nebraska, even though it was not an Army location. He had one year left until he could retire and Ranger quickly approved the location. Ranger was going to do all he could to see this would happen. He owed Max this! Ranger had a close buddy at this Air Force Base who took care of the transfer.

Max tried to keep a low profile at this new assignment, however his physical appearance caught almost everyone's eye. He was six feet two inches tall and weighed around 230 pounds. He was a very strong man, but did not have the bulging cosmetic muscles acquired at a gym. His physical appearance was more attuned to that of a western cowboy in a Zane Grey novel. His blue eyes, military haircut and sunburned skin also sent a message to those who might want to test him. He was a lean, mean, hombre!

The war was over for Max, he just wanted to live life and not do any more killing! However, the peace and tranquility he was enjoying soon was upended when he met a nurse by the name of Myra! He happened to meet her at the entrance to the base hospital. There eyes met and locked on for a brief second. It was just enough time for Max to take a complete inventory of her equipment, and he did not see anything he did not like! He said, "hello", in a clumsy sort of way and tried to continue on with some small talk. She had already detected, when their eyes locked on each other, that he was trying to hit on her. She immediately set Max straight with a disdainful look that told him, "It will never happen!" Max immediately classified her as a reject and didn't log her into his memory.

About a week later, Myra just happened to run into Max at a grocery store. She acted very surprised to see him. However, everything she was saying didn't quite make sense. Max was very good at reading a young girls face and being a bit older and more "experienced", detected exactly what she was thinking!

Max followed Myra out of the grocery store and due to staring at her tight fitting jeans forgot his own groceries! He offered to help load her groceries into the car and then by accident they both turned into each other. What happened next appeared like uncontrolled teenage exploratory sex. A lady walking by said, "Get a room".

They both knew then that they were going to have to deal with this situation. She invited him over to her house and he readily accepted. Myra prepared him dinner and took her time doing it. She wanted him to suffer before he got his "dessert". She found reasons to touch him but always moved away if he reached for her. Myra put Max's mind in a confused state. He found her physical proportions nearly perfect!

After dinner and dessert, they discussed meeting again the following night for dinner. Max said he knew just the place to go, but I want us to meet this time at seven. Myra hesitated, and then said, "yes". The hesitation bothered Max, but he did not say anything. They both kissed goodnight and Max left for his home.

On his drive back to his house, Max kept going over their conversation during the evening. Her hesitation bothered him. He knew she worked for doctor Thorpe and he had heard rumors of his many relationships, nothing is kept secret on a military base. He wondered if she thought Thorpe would find out she was seeing me. Then his thoughts turned to the dark side and wondered how she became a registered nurse by the time she was twenty-one years old. He figured she must be very smart or she had slept her way to the top! He almost ran into a car at the stop-lite because of thinking too hard at his last thought! He had done some repair work at the hospital throughout the year and had met doctor Thorpe. If the doctor saw Myra with him it could be a problem for her. With all this thinking, he figured he earned another two cans of PBR (Pabst Blue Ribbon) when he got home.

Myra and Max met as scheduled. They were going to a very nice restaurant by the Omaha stockyards. He liked the restaurant; it brought back good memories of when he was a boy growing up. When his dad shipped cattle to the market he would go along with his dad to watch the process. If his dad received a good price for the cattle they would eat at this restaurant.

Max noticed something was bothering Myra on the way to the restaurant. He did not try to get to the bottom of it, why waste an evening that was going to cost him plenty? This was not a cheap restaurant!

Little by little, Myra started telling Max things that seemed like classified information. Max was troubled when she told him classified things that came from her boss, because it made him wonder just how close she was with her boss.

During the meal Myra leaned toward Max and confided in him that there was a very dangerous plague causing the deaths of a lot of people in Iraq and that the doctors didn't have a cure for it. Also, they say it was spreading fast. She went on to say that her boss felt that drastic measures would soon be taken all over the world and it would most likely be on the news tomorrow. She concluded that world leaders were meeting at that moment deciding on just what to do. There was also the possibility that some other country might think this plague was made by a rogue country. This could cause a major war!

This information was of interest to Max, but he found it a bit of a stretch that it would make it over here. However, he was concerned that if there were a crisis, especially with their present unstable government, groups like the Soros funded Antifa would try to seize control. Myra was far more concerned about this plague than Max was. She understood the situation from a medical standpoint.

The following day Max was given an assignment to adjust some of the doors in a hangar on base. It was tedious work but just what he needed for some serious thinking. He had just two more days and he would be retired. Once they signed his paperwork he would be a free man. Max decided though that he would not have to immediately leave his apartment because the rent was paid until the end of the month. This would give him some time to spend with Myra, and maybe talk her into living with him, he mused. After some thought, he was not feel confident with the idea that she would live with him. He figured Doctor Thorpe had led her to believe her job was very important and if the plague made it over here she would be working night and day. The idea that she would not be living with him suddenly upset him. He had an unexpected reaction and kicked his toolbox and smashed his fist against the door!

After taking a long walk around the building he got to thinking about the date he was going to have with Myra that night. He was sure she would have a lot more to tell him about the plague. He hoped his plan to take Myra for a picnic at the Platte River would be exciting for her.

Max prepared a number of sandwiches along with a few beers, a couple of sodas and some potato chips. The meal did not look that great, but it was just a picnic.

After cleaning his jeep he returned back to his apartment, cleaned up and put on his best shirt. He also slapped a small amount of cologne on his face, and then determined that she would certainly have a problem resisting him!

The weather was beautiful and the sky contained a few large clouds to keep ones viewing at an elevated level. The outside air blowing upon him as he raced down the road gave him the feeling he was a teenager on his way to pick up his first date. Her house was now in sight!

Chapter 2

A Picnic at The Platte River

When they met up, Max soon became aware that Myra was disturbed. She told him the plague had made it to Denver. He tried to soften the situation by telling her that Denver was a faraway place and he is sure the doctors of the world are working overtime to come up with a cure. It was quickly apparent to Max that his advice did not put her at ease.

It was about a twenty-mile drive to the Platte River. Myra enjoyed the outdoor feeling of the jeep. The temperature was just perfect and the smell of the trees, weeds, wild flowers and the Platte River was something you would never smell in Omaha. The road was empty which also gave one an unspoiled view of the country. Myra was now happy and enjoyed being alone with Max.

Max saw the change in Myra and reached over and put his arm around her shoulder. She leaned toward Max and put her hand on his knee. Now they were both happy! She looked over at Max and saw he was smiling.

It was a small road to get to the river and it was not smooth like the main road. She told Max to slow down and to put both hands on the wheel!

She had never been to the Platte River. Max's jeep allowed them to get fairly close to the water. When they finally picked out the best picnic location they spread the blanket on the grass and placed the picnic items on it.

Max grabbed Myra's hand and encouraged her to walk across the river with him. At one place, the water was waist deep, which concerned Myra a bit, and made her hang on to Max even more. Max explained to her that the water was actually a mile deep in the sand they were walking on. Myra told him that she would always remember their picnic here.

Upon their return to the blanket, they dried off and then indulged in the sandwiches, beer and soda. They watched a beautiful sunset together. For a little while the problems of the world disappeared. Max felt a bond forming with Myra that he had never had with other women.

As the sun was setting, the temperature rapidly cooled down. They wrapped themselves in the blanket and made passionate love. Max got weak at that point and said he wouldn't share her with Doctor Thorpe. Tears flowed from Myra's eyes. They did not talk for a long time. Finally, she turned towards Max and without crying told him she was pregnant. She went on to say that she had just found out and did not know if it was his! She also said she messed up her life just to get an important job and get rich, and that Doctor Thorpe does not know she is pregnant. Myra turned toward Max and told him to hit her and that she deserved anything he did to her.

It was very quiet in the Jeep. Myra's cell phone rang and it was the hospital. She was informed that there were two reported cases of the plague in Lincoln, Nebraska. The whole city was being quarantined until further notice. Max and Myra knew Lincoln was only fifty miles away.

Myra said that starting tomorrow she was to wear a special facemask at all times. She then added that, through the recommendation of Doctor Thorpe, she received a sizeable increase in pay.

Max figured the doctor owned her now. He was angry, and felt sick. He could not stand the image in his head of those two making love. When they parted ways that night, she kissed him goodbye. He did not return the kiss. She began to cry!

Chapter 3

The Plague

The day finally came and Max was released from the military. Also, on that day, three cases of the plague were diagnosed in Omaha. The entire city was put under martial law. The people were scared. On the first day of martial law no one ventured from his or her home, unless it was an emergency and then a special facemask had to be worn. The police and military meant business! The reports coming in from around the country were staggering. One of the cases diagnosed was at Offutt Air Force Base! The good news reported was that medical teams around the world were getting closer to a vaccine. This information took Max totally by surprise. He did not know what to do. He tried to call Myra, but no calls were getting through. Then his cell phone rang. It was Myra. She said she had to see him and that she was at the hospital and was not allowed to leave. Max could tell her voice was not right and she was crying. He told her he was on his way.

Max saw a police car across the street. He ran over to the police car and the policeman pulled a gun on him. Max called him out by name and pulled his mask down far enough so the cop could see who he was. Max kept saying, "It's me, Joe." Joe recognized him and asked how he could help. Max explained that his girlfriend needed him at the hospital and… Joe cut him off and told him to get in the car. It was a hell of a ride to the hospital!

Joe could only drive to about three blocks of the hospital. The streets were full of people thinking they had the plague. It took Max over an hour to get to the entrance. At the hospital Max had some luck. There was a nurse just getting to work and she couldn't make it to the front door. Max told her that he was Myra's boyfriend and that she needed him. The nurse had Max come with her to a side entrance, where they got right in. She also took him to the third floor where she knew Myra was.

The nurse in charge of the third floor took Max to Myra's room. After she let him in, she informed him that he was not allowed to open the door or leave the room and that the doctor would be along shortly. Inside the plastic barrier, Myra laid on a bed. She saw Max and cried out to him. Max sat down next to the bed. They could see each other but could not touch.

Myra told Max that she had taken care of a patient about three days before their picnic at the Platte River. The hospital was unaware the patient had the plague. Myra smiled at Max and told him that he should have come down with it too because they had made love. She felt there was a good chance that he was one of the lucky ones with immunity to the plague.

Max knew that someone would be along soon to take some blood from him to determine if he was carrying the virus.

This was an awful lot for Max to take in. He didn't get to ponder on it for more than 30 seconds and was interrupted by a nurse whom came in to take some blood. She had a mask and gloves on and did not come close to him. Only the needle touched his skin!

In about two hours Doctor Thorpe came in and sat down across from Max. He informed Max that he did not have the virus. He then told Max that he needed some information from him in order to give the doctors that are studying the virus to figure out how it is acquired and transmitted to another party.

The first question was the big one. The doctor wanted to know if he had shared any bodily fluids with Myra when they were on their date at the Platte River. Max answered truthfully and enjoyed the tortured look on the doctor's face. He asked no more questions.

Doctor Thorpe told Max that he should have acquired the plague. Based on their findings, it was determined that Max had a natural immunity to the virus.

Max asked the doctor if he would be able to save Myra. The doctor's reply was chilling. He said there was nothing more that he could do. Myra would have to win this fight all on her own. Max thought about what an extremely strong-willed person she was, and he didn't rule out that possibility.

Max could tell by the expression on the doctor's face and the tone of his voice that he would have loved to lay the blame for all this on him. Max knew the anger the doctor must have felt. He also felt that there should have been better procedures in place for diagnosing patients. How much had the good doctor learned at Myra's expense?

The doctor now did what Max was sure he didn't want to do, he asked Max to stay by Myra until the end or until he got back in the morning. He added that he had not slept in three days and that patients inside and outside the hospital needed his help. Max assured him that he would not leave her.

The doctor needed to leave, but to cover his guilt of not staying with his lover went on to explain about the drip line attached to Myra's arm, which was injecting antibiotics and nutrients into her. He also explained that the air in the hospital contained anti-germ gas. He concluded that there was nothing more that could be done and that the room would remain sealed until he returned tomorrow. He glared at Max and left the room!

Max put his hand on Myra's arm so he could feel her blood moving. He tried to talk to her but there was no reaction. He squeezed her arm harder hoping his strength would be absorbed into her blood veins. He knew what he was doing would not work but, when you're desperate, you do crazy things.

Even as she lay there dying, Myra was beautiful. Max thought about the first time they physically ran into each other while loading groceries into the car. She treated him bad before that moment, but once they touched, they became physically aggressive in showing their desire for each other. It was blind love for Max and Myra. They both had a good laugh at the lady who had walked past them and told them to get a room.

Myra opened her eyes and Max wanted to think she recognized him. However, her eyes quickly closed again. He was absolutely sure there was a different expression on her face now. He tried talking to her again and ran his fingers through her hair, but there was no reaction. He took a firm grip on her arm again, but still no reaction. He was overcome with emotion and wept.

The night air was setting in. The darkness created a feeling of despair. Adding to this despair, Max found the bed to be wet. It took a considerable amount of effort to replace the sheets and her nightgown. Upon completion of these tasks, Max felt her forehead and to his surprise, it was hot! He checked the thermometer control unit and it was blinking a number of 106 degrees. He had not been watching the controls! His mind was in panic mode now. He remembered what his mother had done when he was five years old and very sick. She had put him in a bathtub of cold water.

Max immediately went to the shower and turned the temperature control to cold. He hated cold showers. He took his clothes off and then undressed Myra. After removing the cover from the bed, he carefully picked up Myra and all the wires attached to her and got into the shower. He sat down on a bench in the shower with Myra on his lap. God, it was cold at first, but with her very warm body next to him, it became tolerable. It was eleven p.m.

At four a.m. Myra's fever finally broke. The muscles in his arms did not want to function properly as he tried to get her robe back on. He was incredibly tired. Now Max found some difficulty in getting himself dressed. He finally completed the task and sat down by Myra. He noticed that Myra was looking at him. She didn't say anything but kept on looking at hm. This alarmed him somewhat. He wondered if she recognized him. Then her eyes closed, and she fell back asleep again. He checked her pulse and it felt strong. Max sat there thinking about the voice he heard in the shower. Did he receive help? He did something he had not done in twenty years, he prayed. He said the Lord's Prayer and then just plainly talked to God. He kept on talking, thinking that the more he prayed, the more help God would give.

Max looked over at Myra and her green eyes opened again. She started talking, saying that she had been listening to him praying and that she loved him.

In the morning the doctor returned to find Max asleep on Myra's arm. He looked around the room and wondered who was taking care of who when seeing Myra wide-awake. He then looked at the history of Myra's vital signs on the machine and was alarmed at how high her fever was for almost five hours. He sat down next to them and wanted to know everything that had happened through the night.

Max told the doctor that the devil wanted Myra in the worst way, but she refused to die. He also informed the doctor that he held her in a cold shower for about five hours and I think that broke the fever. I think the devil is not happy today.

Max could tell that the doctor needed him to leave so he could examine Myra. He told the doctor that he was available to help with Myra whenever he was needed. He then gave Myra a kiss and told the doctor goodbye and headed home.

After leaving the hospital Max went straight to his apartment. He drank three cans of ice cold PBR and went to bed. He slept for ten hours and was awakened to a thunderstorm. He loved rainy weather and decided to go for a walk. He did some quality thinking once again. The outcome of all his thinking was that he would never go out on a date with Myra again!

Max also thought about the yelling at God he had done in the shower. He once again tried to make a deal with God, that if God would let her live, he would stay out of her life. All these deals with God got him to thinking about all the deals he had made with God in Afghanistan when he thought he couldn't survive the mess he was in. He knew he had to leave town before he screwed all this up.

On the way back to his house, Max walked past a house that had an Antifa flag hanging from a pole. He momentarily lost it. He went over and ripped the flag off the pole and tore it to shreds. He then threw it on the ground and urinated on it. As Max walked back to the sidewalk, he noticed Joe in his police car across the street. Joe waved at him and drove off. When Max got back to his house he immediately started to pack up his belongings. While he did this, the storm outside intensified. This was no weather to be travelling in and he knew it. He decided to wait until Saturday, which was only three days away.

Max's phone rang, and it was Joe. Joe reminded Max that he was in Afghanistan in the same unit as him. He went on to say that he could see that anger was overwhelming him and that he should talk these things through with Myra. In conclusion, Joe told him that he couldn't keep overlooking the law-breaking things that he was starting to do.

Max thanked Joe for the wake-up call and then went on to say that his TV and everything else he couldn't fit into the jeep were his if he could find him four containers of gasoline. Joe thought that was a pretty good deal. He said good-bye and showed up shortly thereafter at Max's house with four gasoline containers with 'Police Department' written on the side! They both sat down and had a PBR and talked about the good times they had together. Joe shook hands with Max and told him he had to leave.

Just when Max finished packing, there was a knock at the door. It was the doctor. He had no choice but let the bastard in. He said he wanted to talk. Max told him that he would listen to what he had to say but that he was leaving Nebraska at the end of the week.

The Doctor said he understood Max's decision but there was something he felt he needed to tell him. After a pause, the doctor informed Max that his name was in a bunch of medical reports that list people who are immune to the plague. He went on to tell Max that there was most likely a bounty on his head and that it was probably large. There are plenty of desperate, unscrupulous people out there who would want to save their own lives and they would need all his blood. The procedure, the doctor explained, was to drain all the blood from one body and nearly completely replace another body's blood with it. He went on to say that with a single phone call that person could make upwards of fifty million dollars! And just about any doctor or nurse could perform the procedure. To cover their tracks though, they would most likely let you die. In conclusion, the doctor told Max that Myra had informed his wife of their relationship and that action resulted in divorce proceedings. Also, Myra and his wife had gone to the Base General with this, which resulted in the doctor no longer having a job.

After a brief pause, the doctor told Max that his ex-wife and/or Myra, will also cause more legal action to come his way but, for his own benefit, he wanted to see Myra leave town before she does more harm. To encourage her to do so, he had given her one hundred thousand dollars. He hoped this would close the matter and he could go back to being a doctor again. With that comment, the doctor rose from his chair and left.

Max had trouble putting all this information together. The action by Myra against the doctor seemed extreme. There just seemed to be something missing from the story. She had to have been very angry to come up at the strength to have done all of this. Max hesitated for quite a while making up his mind about calling Myra. He was afraid she would tell him to go to Hell! Finally, he called, and Myra answered on the first ring. They both kept talking at the same time. Max finally said he was coming over to her place and he hung up the phone.

On the way to Myra's apartment, Max observed people still waiting in line to get into the hospitals and churches dispensing food and the grocery stores that still had food. However, the lines were shorter than before. This trip was uplifting for him. Everyone seemed more organized. Not a single person was without a mask or gloves. The people were going to beat this plague, and were not giving up!

Max was anxious to tell Myra the news, if she hadn't heard it already, that a vaccine was developed and was in mass production around the world.

The main thought on his mind was problems concerning Myra. She had gone through so much in just a week's time, especially only being twenty-one years old. He felt a heavy load of guilt on his shoulders. He also thought about what the doctor said about wanting Myra to get out of the state. He was not afraid of the doctor in fact ideas of dealing with him kept crossing his mind. An idea to get Myra far away from him was to go to California. He had a cousin named Ron over there, somewhere. After he thought about it he remembered that he had his phone number. He hoped it was still his number and that they still had phone service because of the plague. Max figured he could drive to California in three days if there were no obstacles like gasoline, weather, or Antifa gangs. Gas seemed like the biggest problem, but it may have been solved with the containers Joe had given him. But there was something else that worried Max; he did not have much in common with Ron. Ron was a "do-gooder" and if Max's memory was right, had become a minister!

Myra's apartment loomed ahead so Max shut down his daydreaming. He hurriedly parked the Jeep and ran to the door. Myra must have been watching for Max because the door opened before he got to it. When Max saw her, he was alarmed. She was about twenty pounds less than she was in the hospital. He was afraid to hug her because he thought she might break. They kissed softly and he felt her nails digging into his back. Breathing hard, she pushed Max away and began hitting and screaming at him. Max just stood there, receiving her blows. The more her blows hurt, the better he felt. He deserved it. Little by little, there was less in Myra's blows and then Max realized that he was holding her up. She collapsed into his arms and he carried her to the sofa. He gave her an order to rest while he made dinner. He planned on stuffing her with food!

Max had to wake her when his meal of rotini and chicken soup was ready. They ate at the sofa. She ate well at first but then began to slow down. Max told her that he would force her to eat if she didn't eat the entire meal. She did pretty well but then it all came back up! Puke was something that Max didn't handle very well. He had to make a trip to the toilet where he too lost his meal.

Max decided that there was only one practical thing to do, which was to take a shower with Myra. He thought it would be too dangerous for her to take a shower by herself. When he undressed her on the sofa, he noticed a small incision on her abdomen not there before. The sight of the small incision reminded him of a girl he had once dated who told him she didn't have to worry about getting pregnant!

Max decided to give her a sponge bath only. He decided not to confront her on this because it might be too much for her to deal with right then. Max thought, if the doctor did this to her without her permission, he was going to kill him. Max, shaking with anger, went to the refrigerator and got a PBR and drank it quickly. He needed to calm down. He had to talk to Joe!

Myra was sleeping soundly next to Max on the sofa. He decided this would be a good time to call his cousin, Ron, in California. Max was surprised that his call went right through and that Ron recognized his voice. Max found Ron very easy to talk to, almost like a friend that he had grown up with. By the time Max finished talking, Ron knew everything Myra had gone through. Then it was Ron's turn to talk.

Ron informed Max that he was a minister and that his wife's name was Peng and that they lived in Sausalito. He said that when they had first received news of the plague, the people of his church tried to do their best for the children, so they put them all, along with Peng, in the church and locked the doors! The plan worked well at first. Many of the parents of these children died. Ron, at this point, had to stop and compose himself. He then told Max that an Antifa gang had just burned down the church. He explained how difficult it was to get all the kids to the boat by the marina, without touching them. They did it, but there was a lot of crying parents.

Ron explained to Max that they were considering a plan to take the children to Dutch Harbor on the boat we have them living on now. The owner's son is on board and has sailed this boat many times even though he is only fifteen years old." Ron and some of the parents weren't comfortable with a fifteen-year-old being responsible for twenty children. There was a pause and Ron said that you and Myra could do this. Myra is a nurse and you have done some sailing years ago.

This caught Max by surprise. He was not sure if Myra would be the right person for this task. Max finally told Ron that he would have to talk to Myra and call him back. Ron said he would be waiting for the call and we do want you both to come up here.

Max saw that Myra had been listening to his conversation with Ron. He asked Myra if she would like to go to Sausalito and take a ride to Dutch Harbor. Myra excitedly said she was ready to go and added that she was born in Sausalito and lived there for five years.

Max immediately called Ron and said they were on the way.

Ron gave them a word of caution about the driving conditions on the roads, explaining there was very little law out there now. Also to plan your trip so that you come into Sausalito from the north, because there is no law south of San Francisco and that Antifa is the law in most places now. He concluded with a short prayer and blessed both Myra and Max.

Chapter 4

California Here We Come

Max spent considerable time studying the map to find the best route to Sausalito, California. He finally came to the conclusion that I-80 was the way to go. He figured that if any road would be policed, it would be an interstate highway.

Max changed the oil in the Jeep and also replaced the fan belt. He wanted to make sure that they didn't break down in the middle of nowhere. Just as he finished, he noticed that he needed new windshield wiper blades. They still worked, but were showing wear. Every auto parts store he checked was closed however. Finally, he determined that if a wiper blade broke, it wouldn't shut them down.

Myra was excited about going to California, especially to see Sausalito again. She had left when she was six years old. She could faintly remember the apartment she lived in. It was above a bakery that her mother worked at. Oh, and the Golden Gate Bridge. 'Coming from the north', she thought, 'we will turn left just before the bridge.'

Max, on the other hand, was very concerned about getting to California. Policeman Joe warned him about the hazards on the road. He specifically advised him not to drive at night. He also gave Max four boxes of .45 caliber bullets, which were hard to come by.

Max and Myra sat down together and studied the map. They decided on I-80 until they got to Cheyenne and then they would review the map and the weather and advice from truckers on which way to go after that. They next discussed the fuel problem. Max told her about the extra fuel cans in the Jeep, which Myra felt were very dangerous.

She gave in on the fuel cans and that this fuel would only be used as a last resort. Max told her of the food he had, which was mostly junk food. Myra thought that junk food was not a good diet for them, but they had no choice. Then they went outside to the Jeep to see what room was left. This is when she noticed a case of beer hidden under a case of water. She wanted the beer removed immediately but Max convinced her that they would have to unload almost everything to get the beer out! Once again, Myra lost the battle.

Myra stuffed her suitcase and a bag of blue jeans and a heavy coat into the Jeep. She then called a friend, telling her where the house key was hidden and that everything in the house was hers. Next, being women, they cried for a while and finally said good-bye.

Max found that he left his flashlight at his house so they had to make a final stop. He hurried in to pick it up and, on his way back to the Jeep, he noticed two young men replacing the Antifa flag! He continued to his Jeep, opened the rear door and took out a one inch thick, four-foot-long piece of hickory. He then walked over to the two young men and told them to take the flag down.

Their reply to Max had something to do with his mother. These ugly comments were quickly regretted and followed by screams for mercy. Max liked how he handled the situation. He gave these two pieces of crap a lesson, without killing them.

On the way back to his Jeep, Joe came driving by, shaking his head. Joe pulled over to the curb and walked over to Myra. He introduced himself and said he was Max's best friend and then told her that she was everything Max had told her she was. Then a man yelled out is window something to the effect of thanking Max for doing what he, himself, should have done to the Antifa trash.

When Max got back to his Jeep, emotion was starting to set in amongst the three of them. Joe was not going to have any of that tear and hugging business and told them to be careful and he left. Max felt himself choking up and turned his head so Myra would not see him losing control. A real man does not get emotional!

It was 8 am now and they were on I-80 heading west at about 85 mph. There were very few cars on the road and not once did they see a patrolman.

Myra was still arranging items in the Jeep to give them more room. She noticed Max's .45 and she just stared at it. She asked Max if he would show her how to use it. Max told her that he would train her how to use it, but for right now she shouldn't touch it, because the safety was off!

He pulled off the road at the Columbus, Nebraska turnoff to purchase some gas. They still had over half of a tank but thought it was best to buy gas when they could. Max checked the price on the pump. It was ten dollars a gallon! He walked into the station to make sure of the price. The owner said that it was correct. Max handed him a hundred-dollar bill and said, "Give me ten gallons."

When Max finished at the pump, he noticed there was room for more gas. Well, he was not going to buy it here. The price bothered him even more when the engine started sputtering from time to time, which meant that the crooked owner was watering down his gas!

Max informed Myra that even with a small amount of water in the tank, they would still be able to maintain their speed. He wanted to maintain his speed during the daytime and especially when there was this little traffic.

Myra was becoming a good navigator. She determined that they should get gas at North Platte or Ogallala. She was good at keeping conversation going so Max would not become sleepy.

There was a long expanse of driving for the next few hours. Max thought this was a good time to discuss the scar on her stomach. He confronted her with it and she replied that Doctor Thorpe didn't want to have children and while she was unconscious, he performed an operation that would prevent her from having children. I confronted the doctor and he showed me my signature on a consent form. It was my signature but I don't remember signing that. I showed this document to his wife and a document showing that my body had aborted the baby when I had a 106-degree fever.

Myra said she took a copy of these documents to the commanding General at the base. Another nurse at the hospital helped me do this because I was too weak at the time. She did not think Thorpe would ever be a doctor again. She admitted to having sex with him and it was not consensual! He begged her not to report it or quit. She was young and needed the job and she was stupid. The baby that was aborted was Max's baby and it died during the fever.

Losing his job and his family had punished Thorpe, and losing the baby had punished Myra. She thought Thorpe hated the idea that she was carrying your baby. She told Max that if I had told you this before we left Omaha, you would have killed him and I would have lost you too!

Max drove on for another ten miles and then told Myra that all humans are flawed creatures. The older we get, the more baggage we have to carry. I wake up some nights seeing vivid pictures of enemy soldiers that I have executed. My anger can sometimes overwhelm me. If you hear me crying in bed late at night, wake me up and help me get out of the nightmare. It might be well that we talk to Ron about our problems separately.

Late at night, Max would siphon gas out of cars without owners along the interstate. Myra did not agree with the practice, but rationalized that the owner was most likely dead anyway. Max tried to train her how to siphon gas and it did not work very well. She puked for some time and also cursed Max out for some time. She also had bad breath for some time!

The sun was low in the sky as Max and Myra entered the outskirts of North Platte, Nebraska. Max pulled into a large, mostly empty truck stop. There was only one truck being fueled. The driver had his face covered and was wearing gloves. The gas was reasonably priced, considering the crisis at hand.

While the machine pumped the gas, Max talked to the truck driver. He said that North Platte had been hit very hard by the plague. It was his opinion that the city officials waited too long to implement measures to control the situation. There were so many dead that procedures were being set up to start burning the bodies the next day. To help alleviate the situation, the governor of Nebraska had said that the people of North Platte would be the first to receive the vaccinations in the state.

Chapter 5

Heading for Cheyenne

Max asked the truck driver parked next to him at the gas station if he thought that this would be a safe place to sleep. The truck driver told him that no place was safe after the sun went down. He said that he was heading to Cheyenne and that Max could follow him. He also said that he was well armed and would smash through any non-governmental roadblock they came across. Max agreed and told him that they would be covering his back door and that they were ready to go. Myra was listening to the conversation and moved over to the driver's seat.

Myra yelled to Max that she was driving and wanted him to get some rest. She was excited about driving, especially since the trip was starting to feel like a Mad Max movie. As soon as Max got into the Jeep, they were off. It took Max a while to get comfortable in the reduced space that had been allotted for Myra.

Max warned Myra not to get too close to the truck they decided to follow because he might have to stop very quickly. He gave her a lot of driving instructions until she finally told him to, "Go to sleep!"

The sky was overcast and there was no moon. It was good driving with very few cars to be seen. Max could not sleep so they talked about some articles they had read on the Internet. The story of greatest interest was the sighting of George Soros and Warren Buffet, both of whom had died some thirty years ago. The story that received the most attention was the sighting of Hitler! Very few people took stock in that, however, it was a reputable person that made the sighting. There was also a story/conspiracy theory that both Soros and Hitler were behind the Antifa group. The argument held some water because Soros did work for the Third Reich at one time.

Myra pointed out that these stories were reported more often in the past couple years and a considerable number of people think there may be something to this red pill, which was keeping these people alive. She added that a lot of the people thought it was not fair that the rich or elites could afford the red pill and they could not.

Max said that he had watched a program on TV that said the red pill costs a million dollars and that you had to take one every six months.

Myra interjected that the pill doesn't make you young again; it just slows the aging process.

They were both tiring of the small talk and Max finally fell to sleep. Myra was not paying attention and was driving close to the truck. All of a sudden, the truck exploded. Myra slammed on the breaks and Max slid to the floor. They both unbuckled their seatbelts and got out to see what had happened.

Max determined that the truck had tried to ram through a roadblock of two cars sitting sideways on the road. There were two guys lying dead on the left side and one on the right was reaching for his gun. Max dispatched him with his.45. Myra observed all of this, especially the cold, calculated way that Max had shot the man reaching for his gun. This bothered her a little and she wondered about this man she had fallen in love with. He appeared to be the judge, jury and executioner.

Max placed a few flares on the road. They both got back into the Jeep and continued their journey. Myra asked if the truck driver was dead and Max told her that he had been burned beyond recognition. He also noted that they would be out of gas in about half an hour.

Myra didn't say anything else for some time. She was a little concerned at how calm and cool Max was after killing someone.

Max pulled into the next rest area. There were no cars to be seen. They both got out of the Jeep. Max opened the rear door and pulled out a five-gallon tank of gas along with a funnel. He handed his .45 to Myra because it was in his way when he was pouring the fuel.

Myra looked toward the building in the rest area and was startled to see two men dressed in black, running right at them with clubs. They were only fifty feet away. She started screaming and emptied the .45 at them. The gun was way to large and had too big a kick for her to handle. She missed with every shot. The two men were so scared because of the bullets whizzing past them that they dropped their clubs and ran. Max ended up pouring a gallon of gas on his jeans!

He had to pry the .45 out of Myra's hands. She also had to change her jeans! All Max said was, "How could you miss at that range?" After a few deep breaths, Max informed her that she had saved their lives, which made her feel quite proud.

Finally, they made it to Cheyenne. Max did a lot of sleeping. Myra, on the other hand, stayed awake and periodically looked at the .45 sitting by her leg.

Myra pulled in to a truck stop and next to a pump. She woke her sleeping baby and told him where they were. Max got out of the Jeep and stretched a bit and filled the tank. Myra put her gloves and mask on and headed for the ladies' room. They had decided at the start of the trip that they would never leave the Jeep alone!

Max began to worry about Myra being gone so long. He locked up the Jeep, stuck the .45 in his belt and went inside the store. The clerk at the counter was playing on his cell phone and not paying attention to the noise down the hall. Max was now running and saw a biker trying to push open the door to the ladies' room. He could also hear Myra screaming for help. Max pulled out his .45 and smashed it against the startled biker's face. The biker quickly backed up, he did not want any more of that.

Myra quickly opened the door and demanded that Max give her the gun. Max said no and told her to get back to the jeep. As Myra ran to the jeep, she could hear more groans from the biker!

When they got into the Jeep, Max said that from now on, they would go to the bathroom together. He also added, with a grin, that she was a nurse and had seen it all before anyway.

Myra did not think that was funny and looked down at the .45 and saw all the blood on it. She went right to work cleaning the gun and when finished, put it closer to her than to Max, as if to say that she had taken ownership of the gun!

Max took over driving and informed Myra that the next stop would be Rock Springs. Because there were no cops on the road, Max set the cruise control at 85 mph. He sure wanted to be in Utah before dark.

Myra pulled out a gallon can of peanuts and set them between her and Max. She also gave him what he wanted, a PBR. She stayed with water. The scenery and the smell of the pines were awesome. She was enjoying the trip.

Even with the cruise control set at 85 mph, a car came up behind them. It looked like they had to brake to not hit us. Max was not sure what was going on. He tried slowing down but the other car slowed down too. The game stopped when Max brought down the speed to zero. Max quickly stepped out of the Jeep and pointed his .45 at them. They reversed and backed up at full speed. The driver overcorrected at that speed, lost control and ended up in the ditch.

Max got back in the Jeep and put the .45 next to Myra. It appeared to Myra that the .45 sure helped people change their minds without even having to shoot them.

The miles and time clicked away and at 4 pm, they rolled into an empty gas station at Rock Springs, Wyoming. This time, Max went inside for a refreshing stop. Max noticed there were some fresh hotdogs for sale. He purchased four of them. The clerk had quite a time handling them with her gloves. Max gave her a fifty and told her to keep the change. He asked her how safe the roads were going west. She told him that there was no law west of the Utah border!

Max hurried back to the Jeep. Myra had taken care of the fueling and was sitting behind the wheel, ready to go.

Myra noticed that Max was checking over the .45, making sure the clip was full, etc. She asked him why he was checking the gun and he said the clerk tipped him off that there could be trouble after they crossed the Utah border. He now, very much wanted to be in California the next day.

Max told Myra that it would be nice to have a bench seat like the old cars used to have so she could sit next to him. I get pretty lonely over here. My dad said that when he was young, fifty percent of the firstborn were conceived in the front seat of a pickup truck. He went on to say that if he got sleepy in the Jeep, she could do nothing to help him stay awake.

Myra was quick to tell Max that he was a sick man! By the time they crossed the Utah border, she could tell that Max appeared tired. It was then that Myra attempted the impossible. This almost caused Max to drive off of the road!

Max suggested that Myra take over driving at the next stop. And if it looked real safe, maybe we could stop for an hour and get out and run around the Jeep a bunch of times to get our blood flowing again.

At Salt Lake City, Max turned into a large truck stop. They were surprised to see uniformed people in the yard making sure that everyone had gloves on and were wearing masks. They meant business! They even asked Max and Myra where they were going. The agent that dealt with them said 50,000 federal troops had been deployed to California and the governor had been placed under house arrest.

They felt an urgency now to get to Sausalito. They put on gloves and masks and filled up, then went inside to refresh.

On the TV inside the gas station, the President of the United States was speaking. He declared that the Antifa gangs were now being considered, terrorists, and the money left in a fund by the late George Soros; to aid Antifa would be taken by the federal government. He concluded his speech saying that the governments around the world will find out the origin of the plague and added that preliminary findings indicate that it didn't start in Iraq.

Myra and Max got back on the road. They kept the radio on a news channel for the rest of the trip. There was snow falling now in the higher passes. It would not be long and they would be in California. Myra said that they should refuel before they get to the Sierra Nevada's, just in case a snowstorm blocks them. There was a clean looking gas station ahead and they quickly fueled up. They did not go inside to refresh. They were anxious to get to California.

When they approached Donner Pass, the snow became heavy. Max and Myra became very concerned. Max shifted the Jeep into four-wheel-drive and slowed down to around 40 mph for the next hundred miles. Their good gas mileage slipped a bit in the high, cold altitude and they had to use the last can of gas.

While fueling, neither Max nor Myra noticed the pickup that pulled in behind them. They heard the truck door slam shut in the wind and then saw two bad looking men approaching them. Max went for his gun in the Jeep and Myra went for the passenger door. Myra was too slow and was grabbed. The grab was also in a bad place! She was quickly released when they saw the .45.

Now it was the bad looking men's turn to hurry. They scampered to get into their truck. As a safety, Max shot one of their tires. Max returned to the Jeep and they were off.

Myra had a greasy smudge mark on her blouse. Her language turned downright bad. She took her blouse off and crawled into the back of the Jeep to get to her clothes. When she got back to her seat, she noticed that Max was grinning! She asked Max why he didn't shoot them. There was no reply from Max.

The news program on the radio warned able bodied men and women that ask for welfare for themselves and have no job will be given a job with the military. The military was in much need of recruits. The plague had depleted their ranks considerably. The plague was extremely hard on the military because they had to get in there and help the people.

Chapter 6

San Francisco Here We Come

The sun was setting now as they read the mileage sign. It said 80 miles to San Francisco. Max pulled over to the side of the road to study the map. He remembered that they should come from the north and turn left before they got to the Golden Gate Bridge. Max decided to call Ron just to make sure which road to take. Ron was very happy to hear Max's voice. He went over the route to take and also informed him that there were soldiers everywhere, and that they are the law! They don't tell anyone anything twice. You would not want to be an Antifa person around here.

Then Ron said, "You might find this hard to believe but the governments of all the Latin American countries are begging for their people to come back from America. They need people to run their factories, etc." He then said, "We can talk later when you get here, just get here safe and sound." Max was glad there were few cars on the road because the route to Sausalito was getting complicated. And then there it was ahead of them, the Golden Gate Bridge! In their excitement, they almost missed their turnoff for Sausalito. Myra knew that she must look terrible. She needed a shower in the worst way. Max informed her that they could not stop for a shower.

Max and Ron did not recognize each other when they met. In fact, Max drove right on by, but when Ron saw the Nebraska license plates, he ran down the street after them. The greetings took a long time. Ron had two teenagers and they had heard big stories about Max's exploits in

Afghanistan and about Myra surviving the plague. Max hoped that Ron hadn't told them too much, especially the teenagers, Matt and Andrew.

Max and Myra did not know what to expect with Ron and his wife Peng. For some reason, Max had never asked what her name was nor did Ron ever tell him that she was Chinese. It was a little clumsy at first but soon they were all very close.

Ron informed Max that one of the three sailboats docked down there is his new home. After one year, if the original owner didn't furnish the proper paperwork, it becomes yours. We will go down tomorrow and sign some papers for a claim on the boat.

Ron went on to say that there were quite a few cars, boats and homes that have no owners. The owners had all most likely died from the plague. Also, Ron said that they could buy a $100,000 bond at the courthouse and take ownership of the marina and the remaining two boats. If the rightful owner showed up, they would get their $100,000 back and at some point, if no one showed up, it would become Max and Myra's. Ron would do it but he didn't have that kind of money.

Myra jumped into the conversation and said that she had the money and that it was in the Jeep. Myra noticed that Max had gone into shock. She went on to say that she was not going to take any chances on a man until he married her. Everyone but Max was laughing at this point.

Ron saw a possible problem here. With Max not laughing and said that marriage is not a sacrament in the church. Baptism is, but not marriage. All a man and a woman have to do is solemnly swear to each other that they are in love, and I'm sure you two, in so many words, have done that. Now, anytime you want a church blessing before all the people in church, I will be more than happy to be your minster and take care of it. I do, however, charge a small fee.

Ron's two teenagers, Matthew and Andrew, were amazed at this strong-willed Myra. They certainly were taking a liking to her. Their mother, Peng, was far more submissive to their dad and they could not quite imagine their mother with $100,000. Myra's blond hair and figure were interesting too, not that they were staring. They were very careful about that. A conversation on this topic with their mother would not be very pleasant.

Peng had a Chinese meal prepared for everyone. They all must have been tired or hungry because the talking slowed down abruptly. Myra noticed that Matt sat on one side of her and Andrew sat on the other. Peng noticed it also.

They lived near their church, which was two blocks away. Peng noticed Myra looked very tired and suggested that they come to church tomorrow and then spend the entire afternoon together and make plans for the week. They all thought that was a good idea.

Ron said that he would have to be excused because he had to plan his sermon for the next day. Peng escorted Myra to her room. Max said he wanted to walk around the pier area and unwind after the trip.

Max gazed at the lights of San Francisco and the Golden Gate. It started to drizzle a bit and that made it even more beautiful. He felt safe here with his friends. He decided to turn around, because of the drizzle and head back to Myra.

Myra had already finished her shower when Max returned. She had slipped some clean clothes on and wrapped a towel around her hair. She told Max that she wanted to sit outside for a bit. And she also added that she just put the $100,000 in the hanging clothes hangar/suitcase. She also iced down his last PBR in the bathroom sink. She thought that Ron may not allow drinking here and told Max to make sure he hid the can after he drank it.

Chapter 7

Sausalito

In the morning, Matt took everyone to a farmer's market for breakfast, before they went to church. There was a selection of crappy organic food and then there was the coffee and pancakes. Everyone ordered the coffee and pancakes.

Andrew had his radio on while they ate. The commentator on the station Andrew was listening to told of another sighting of George Soros, this time in the New York City area. The person said that there was no picture or autograph of Soros and there was only one person who claimed to have actually seen him.

This radio station was known for starting the conspiracy theory that a number of people alive today were once connected to the Third Reich. It was suggested that they were the ones who were supporting Antifa and many globalists to rule the world. It is generally noted that at least ten percent of the people worldwide believe this conspiracy theory.

Naturally, the commentator next went to the discussion of the U-977 and U-530 that escaped to Argentina after the war. The question is always discussed, did the people in these U-boats discover, amongst the natives, the secret ingredient of the red pill. If the red pill existed at that time, Hitler and Soros and many of their compadres could still be alive!

Matt had a different station on, which dealt more with what was happening in the state and the nation. The commentator said that the economy had decreased by some 75% compared to last year and also that all car factories had shut down. There was zero demand for new cars now. If you needed a car, you just went out to the street and got one that no longer had an owner! He concluded that the banks had been closed down for thirty days and the government had devalued our money by fifty percent.

Everyone was surprised by what they had just heard on Matt's radio. The boys were old enough to understand these issues. They looked to the adults for answers but they had none.

The people at the church were very solemn. Ron did his best to uplift the people with music. The people were mad at their government. Most people in California were dependent on the government. They wanted free stuff. Now they had to quickly learn how to do it for themselves.

Ron suggested that they add a Wednesday church service, because a week is just too long to wait if something went wrong and needed more immediate attention. He went on to say that they needed a plan to educate children, because the schools were still not running, and they had no doctors in the city. These are some of the problems he wanted to deal with at the Wednesday meetings.

Myra stood, introduced her and Max and said that she was a registered nurse and would be setting up a clinic in the marina.

Max then stood and said that he needed up to eight students to fish with him every day out in the ocean on his sailboat. A number of kids got loose from their parents and went directly over to Max.

These things that Max and Myra said cheered the group up considerably. There was hope in the air! The older boys and girls were eager to go fishing on his sailboat. Unfortunately, the weather was rainy all week. Most of the kids had only one parent because of the plague. Some of them were living in houses by themselves. Max and Myra were unaware of these problems. Even the military was spread thin and most of the soldiers hadn't been through basic training. Whenever there was a problem in the Sausalito area, the military would arrive late or not at all.

Max spent the week fortifying his 45-foot sailboat. He wanted to have safe areas that could withstand bullets. No one understood what he was doing except himself. Basically, he fortified the stairwell and the fuel tank. He knew that a one-inch thick board would not stop a bullet, but the wood, along with a mattress may do the job.

If Myra or any of the other parents involved with the fishing project knew or understood the danger that Antifa posed, they would have shut down the project. This worried Max too, but they needed the fish. Some of the people in church gave the appearance of starving.

The leaders of Antifa forces gave out orders to burn all pleasure boats and marinas because, they were most likely owned by rich people. Max was aware of this! He decided that his handgun was not adequate enough if war came to this community.

In one of the empty cars that Max was syphoning gas from, he saw a rifle on the floor in the backseat. He looked around and determined that the street was empty. He then broke the window and retrieved the rifle. It was an M-14, which was used by the military fifty years ago and still today as a sniper rifle. The rifle looked to be in good condition but he could only find eight rounds. That would never do!

He thought long and hard on where to get more ammunition. Finally, he decided to ask the parishioners at church and see what they could come up with. Max followed up on his plan and told everyone that he sometimes had to shoot sharks when he was out fishing. Everyone seemed to buy into his lie.

An elderly daughter of a deceased military sniper said that she had at least a thousand rounds and had wanting to get rid of them for a long time. Max took them off her hands and she thanked him. Max considered this only a partial lie and would probably be able to slip it past Saint Peter someday.

Ron thought this all sounded a bit fishy but had too many of his own problems to worry about.

Myra was busy by now, setting up a clinic in the marina. Word got around about a clinic and people that used to their church started showing up. Myra wrote to the county medical office for approval and guidance on this clinic of hers. She also gave them her Nebraska credentials. She soon received a message back that she was free to do whatever she wanted after reviewing her credentials. They also added that they would do anything they could to help her because of the crisis going on in the country right now. She felt the county would have no choice. About a week later a bunch of basic supplies were received from the county. She also found out later that the hospital in Omaha at Offutt Air Force Base gave her a tremendously good rating!

Max and a number of the teenagers finally went fishing and were very successful. Everyone was tired and sore when they returned to the marina. Fred came over to the marina and helped train everyone in how to clean fish. Word very quickly got out and quite a few people had fish for dinner that night.

The fishing was short lived for the week, as the rain and wind moved back in. However, the teenagers knew how to fish and some activity took place off the peers and the coastline. They soon found out that the Golden Gate Bridge was too high to fish from!

Fred was soon put in charge of organizing fishing outings. These outings were always off a bridge or peer or rocks along the coast. No one in the area was starving anymore. And Fred was experiencing the best time of his life. He was an idle to the teenagers. Fred could see the affect he had on the teenagers and watched his language very carefully. Too many of the young people no longer had parents and looked to Fred for direction.

Chapter 8

The Battle of the Marina

About a week later the following message was attached to her clinic:

CLOSE THIS CLINIC OR WE WILL BURN IT DOWN

Myra was alarmed when she saw the note on the door. She went straight to Max and asked him for the .45.

Max was very upset now and knew Myra needed protection. He could not be standing beside her at all times. He decided that she needed a gun, but not the .45. He decided to check with some guys he met late at night a while back when he was syphoning gas. He left word with one of them that was hanging around the neighborhood. He said to this guy, no name given, that the clinic was receiving threats from Antifa people and the nurse at the clinic needs a 9 mm pistol and a box of bullets. He told the guy that she wouldn't be running from Antifa!

The following day, there was a box at the door of the clinic. Myra had Max check to make sure it wasn't a bomb. She knew that Max had handled many bombs in Afghanistan and he would know what to do.

Max checked the box and opened it. Inside were five new Barrettes (nine millimeter pistols) and five boxes of bullets. No note or letter was in the box. Max now knew they were no longer alone in fighting Antifa. He gave Myra a gun and told her that they would practice later that night.

Max had decided back in Nebraska that he would fight Antifa; he was not going to be forced by global elitists how he was going to live his life. Antifa, which was funded in part by George Soros money, would not destroy this great country!

They both lamented on all that had happened since they met back in Omaha. And then they laughed when they reminisced about their first encounter while they were loading groceries into the car. They almost tore each other's clothes off in the parking lot! They remembered a lady telling them to "Get a room!" They decided to walk over to the outside eating area of a restaurant near the water. The restaurant was not open due to the plague. It was a little chilly out and a mist/fog was moving in. Myra moved close to Max to stay warm.

Max said he heard on the radio that they have determined the first case of the plague actually occurred in a tributary of the Amazon, not Iraq. There was also another item on the news that fed into these conspiracy theories that they had talked about at breakfast. There was a car accident in Argentina. The driver died and he looked strange. He was driving an expensive Mercedes with no registration. Also, he had no identification on him. He had a tie clasp with a Swastika on the back of it and his shoes were all leather and polished. And the real strange thing was that even though he was old, he had baby teeth emerging. He was also carrying a Lugar. They found a red pill in his pocket. Could that be the red pill talked about in the conspiracy theory?

Myra hoped that Matt and Andrew were not listening to the radio because that would be all they would hear about the next day.

Max agreed and also said that those are two sharp and interesting boys. The lights of Alcatraz were visible now. They noted that there were only two other couples sitting out in the eating area next to the water. This place used to be very occupied.

Max noticed two guys dressed in black walking rather fast on the sidewalk some 30-40 feet away. He nudged Myra to alert her. She did not quickly turn around or jump up, but with very smooth motions, reached down and picked up an empty soda bottle. Max reached for his .45, but to his dismay, he didn't have it with him!

Max now noticed that those two guys in black changed direction and one of them carried a backpack. When they were close, Max went into action. The two Antifa men went after Max, writing off the frail woman. The backpack missed its target but Max's knee did not! His partner went for Max's back with a knife, but it fell out of his hand when a bottle came crashing down on his head.

Max and Myra were amazed that the elderly couple sitting a few benches away came over and said they would help slide the two Antifa men off of the pier. When they got near the edge, the elderly couple said they would take it from here. Max felt the offer strange but was okay with it. He wanted to get Myra to safety anyway.

Max and Myra thanked them and started to walk away. Myra happened to glance back and saw the elderly man slit their throats, causing blood to gush out before they were pushed into the water. They both then spit at the dead bodies. Even though Myra was a nurse, she threw up all over the sidewalk. Her knees became weak and Max grabbed her just in time.

Later, on their walk back to the boat, Myra exclaimed to Max that they really make a great team. Max agreed and he pointed out the difference between them and Ron and Peng. Max explained that he saw Peng as an extension of Ron, and we make our own decisions. Note how you shot at the two men at the rest stop, and me shooting the men who blew up that truck. I think I like our arrangement, because there is no hesitation.

When they returned to their sailboat, they sat down on the deck and talked some more. Myra said that she found it interesting that the man that died in the car accident in Argentina was carrying a Lugar pistol and a Swastika tie clasp. Do you think it can be true?

Max said it was startling to me he had baby teeth and the red pill. I heard on that station the red pill stops you from aging. I just don't think I would want to live hundreds of years with all those teeth. What if I took the red pill and you didn't? I would outlive you and become very lonesome.

With that comment, Myra playfully started to torment him until he asked for forgiveness.

Myra wondered if Andrew and Matt were listening to the radio today. She hoped they did not hear the red pill story because if they did, she would have to hear about it all day.

Max and Myra retired early. At about midnight, Max heard a noise outside and smelled smoke. When he got topside, he saw three people dressed in black on the first boat in the line-up. They were pouring gas down the stairwell. The sails were already burning. Max, carrying his .45 and rifle went to work. They did not know Max was sleeping on one of the boats.

He quickly picked one of them off with the .45. Another jumped into the water and tried to get back on at the rear of the boat. Two more people in black were coming to aid their comrades. They both got on the boat but foolishly went down the stairwell where all the gas had been poured. Max's next shot set the stairwell on fire. As best as he could determine, there was only one left.

Max put the rifle down and keeping the .45 in his hand, untied the boat from the pier. The tide was going out and he wanted the boat to head for open water and ride the tide to the ocean. Max jumped on the boat and attempted to steer it away from the other boats. Myra, being very stealthy, got onto the boat that was tied next to the boat that Max was on. She could see Max struggle with another man and the boat was slowly moving out into the open water. She put the Berretta in her pants and jumped in the water. She swam as fast as she could but was not in shape and was tiring fast! Max had his hands full and did not know Myra was in trouble.

Ron and the rest of the family were just out for a walk and seeing the smoke, tried to figure out what was going on. Matt and Andrew figured the swimmer was Myra and they broke away from Ron and Peng and were churning water like you would not believe possible.

Andrew actually reached Myra first and finally had to grab her by the hair before she pulled him both under. Ron and Peng were in the water now too. They all did what they could and got Myra back onto the pier. Andrew immediately started giving her mouth-to-mouth resuscitation. Ron jumped into a rowboat and headed for the burning boat.

Peng soon felt Andrew was working too hard at what he was doing and she took over. Myra started to spit up water and soon came back to life. Peng felt the gun concealed on Myra. When she thought Andrew was not looking, she pulled the gun out and put it in her purse.

However, Andrew did see what his mother had done! He totally admired Myra, in fact, he was in love with her. He took his mother aside and made her promise not to tell Myra what he had done.

Peng was puzzled and told Andrew that he saved her life. She assured him that Myra would be very proud of him. Later that night, Andrew would have the best dream he had ever had in his life. He was certain that he became a man overnight.

Just when Ron caught up with the sailboat, Max jumped off and swam for the rowboat. They both sat there exhausted. Finally, Max told Ron to look at the burning sailboat that was drifting away from them. Max then told Ron that he was observing a Viking funeral for four Antifa soldiers. Ron had realized that the four men had died and in fact, did say some words over their demise. Years later, he would give a sermon about that Viking funeral he had officiated over!

They took turns rowing. It took a while getting back because the tide was going out. After arriving back at the pier, they all hugged each other and then they all decided to sleep on Max and Myra's boat that night. Andrew and Matt were given the task of standing guard.

Max assigned Matt and Andrew to sit on top of the marina roof as lookouts. Every now and then he would check on them to see if they were doing their jobs. Sometimes teenage boys get distracted easily. While on the roof, Matt said that he saw movement on the street to the left, almost eight blocks away but he was having trouble focusing the binoculars.

Andrew said that he knew best how to use the binoculars and took them from Matt. After focusing a bit, Andrew said, "Oh, shit!" There were eight Antifa on the sidewalk on the right side of the road about eight blocks away.

Max immediately did a look-see and agreed. He called Myra and told her to get Ron and Peng and to come back to the marina. He gave them each a Berretta and showed them how to use it. Then told them to find a secure place and only to shoot if Antifa makes it to the marina!

Max sent Andrew and Matt down to Myra as well. Matt brought Max's .45 to give to Myra. Soon, the Antifa were in range for Max's rifle. He started picking them off. Then Max saw another ten or so Antifa arriving.

Max could hear his .45 going off now, frequently. Soon, he heard Barrettas firing off from many different positions. It was encouraging to hear all the guns going off in the marina but he feared that they weren't hitting anything.

The Antifa soldiers soon figured out who knew how to shoot and who didn't. Every time Max raised his head, a bullet whizzed by him. To his amazement, when he looked this time, he was shocked to see old man Fred walking down the middle of the street with his 12-guage shotgun making quite a mess of the Antifa soldiers. They were soon throwing their guns down and surrendering with their hands in the air. Unfortunately for them, Fred did not understand this whole surrender thing and laid waste to them all. The smell of gunpowder filled the air.

Myra came running out of the marina to an Antifa soldier that she saw was still moving on the ground. The soldier was small and she feared that it was only a child. She threw herself over the soldier so Max or Fred did not perform another execution.

Within minutes, Max was there to finish off the soldier. Myra pleaded with him not to do it. Max obeyed her but she could see he didn't like it.

To Myra's surprise, the wounded soldier was a girl. She was fighting for her life and she was screaming in Mandarin. Myra yelled for Peng. Peng, not knowing how she could help, quickly arrived on the scene. She understood everything the soldier was saying and told Myra the girl does not want her throat slit.

Now Ron appeared on the scene and picked up the girl while Myra and Peng held her hands and feet tight. They soon had the girl on the table in the clinic.

Myra injected something into her arm and she very quickly passed out. Myra carefully examined her and found a bullet hole in her back. The bullet went in very deep and could not be reached with a probe. Myra called everyone over to discuss the situation. She informed them that only a surgeon could save her. Run suggested that Max call the Army to see if they could meet us on the Golden Gate Bridge and help get the wounded girl to a hospital.

Max yielded to the three people staring at him. He fumbled through his wallet for a number he had acquired on a patrol he made near the far end of the Golden Gate Bridge a while back. A sniper's bullet almost got him on that patrol, something he never told Myra about.

It took Max about an hour to reach this Army Ranger. He was shocked to find that this was his military boss in Afghanistan. They did not have time to talk but would certainly get together later. He told Max that he could meet him and Myra in the middle of the bridge at midnight. He said that the Antifa snipers don't have scopes making them ineffective at night. He added that it would still be dangerous but the personnel carrier should stop the bullets they would be shooting at them. Max told him they would see him at midnight.

Now it was Max's turn to chair the meeting. There were no questions, just orders. Ron was to drive his car to the meet point after he blesses this whole project. Myra, of course, would stay close to the wounded girl. Peng would be there for translating purposes. Max did not say what he would be doing. He just strapped his .45 on and put a new clip in his M-14. He said that everyone needed to carry a Barretta somewhere on them. He walked over to Ron and told him to get a hold of Fred to be with his sons and to bring his 12-guage.

They only had an hour to get the girl wrapped up and the rest to get their weaponry gathered up and checked out. The hour went fast. They all got into Ron's car and with the lights off, headed to the meet point on the Golden Gate Bridge.

Peng was rattling away in Mandarin and every once in a while, an English word would pop out. It was not a good conversation with who ever she was talking to. Ron was going to have to say a lot of prayers for her when all this was over!

When they got to the meet point, Ranger was already there. Max greeted Ranger with a handshake and then asked Ranger if one of his soldiers could go back with Ron to guard the marina while they were gone, which would be about two or three days. Ranger gave Ron three soldiers and some automatic rifles.

Ron took Peng aside and they hugged and said a short prayer together. Ron did not like the idea of Peng being left in harm's way. After a final kiss, Ron and the soldiers got into the car and drove to Sausalito.

The rest of them got into an eight-wheeled personnel carrier and made for the checkpoint on the bridge. The guard at the checkpoint waved them through. Ranger said it was almost twenty blocks to the Army compound, which also included a hospital.

About three blocks from the checkpoint, the sound of bullets hitting the personnel carrier started concerning everyone. Another armored vehicle arrived on the scene and escorted them to the hospital. A number of Antifa soldiers jumped onto the street with automatic weapons to stop the armored vehicle. This was a big mistake for the Antifa soldiers.

The noise woke the wounded girl and she started screaming and trying to get away. The girl must have scratched Peng's arm. They did not notice the blood at first but when it was discovered, several of them had blood on them when they arrived at the hospital and opened the rear door. The nurses immediately thought the worst and yelled for more help. In short order though, these medical professionals had the wounded girl on the operating table.

The x-ray showed the bullet lodged very close to her heart. The bullet was of a small caliber, most likely from a small caliber Barretta handgun. To note, this wounded girl was the only soldier that made it to the steps of the marina!

The doctor informed the group that the bullet must come out. He added that the outcome was not guaranteed and they should not get their hopes up.

They took her to the operating table and immediately prepped her for surgery. Due to a shortage of nurses, Myra had to assist. It was quite a delicate operation. Two doctors and Myra worked tirelessly clamping veins they cut, etc. to get near the bullet. In the end, they were successful and exhausted. The girl slept for ten hours. No one else slept until she woke up.

It would have been tragic for everyone if she had died because at the end they were all shooting at her to stop her from getting into the marina. Max said later that if she had made it into the marina, it would have been a circular firing squad with bullets going everywhere.

Later in the day, the group met with the doctor in charge. He informed them that she would be able to be moved in a few days, in fact, she could probably walk on her own if she was careful. Then the doctor brought something up they knew nothing about. The girl had a small tattoo on her neck. The tattoo indicated that she was an Antifa soldier. Also, she was most likely used as a whore for the soldiers. The doctor added that there were a number of problems. The first problem he discovered after I talked to her is that she planned to die when she charged the marina. She is afraid that her relatives back in China will find out she was a whore. She is also afraid that if she did not do well as a soldier, they would have made her a whore again. He concluded that at present time, she was a mental basket case.

After a pause, the doctor found the courage to tell them that she wouldn't be able to stay. His fear was that if one of the many soldiers visiting the hospital saw her tattoo, they would come up with a plan to kill her and, in all likelihood, that soldier would be rewarded with a three-day pass and a couple hundred dollars. He also said that you all might find this practice distasteful, but it's helping us win the war. He added that she is very scared of Antifa getting ahold of her and putting her back to work as a whore. We cannot keep her here, as she must be guarded all the time. Maybe Peng can get through to her to explain what is going on. Peng is the only one who speaks Mandarin right now. You all have two days to come up with a plan.

Chapter 9

The Battle of Berkeley Hills

Max set up a meeting with Ranger to discuss a plan. When they met, Ranger informed Max that he couldn't get them safely across the Golden Gate Bridge at this time. Antifa had moved a thousand or so troops to the area. But I can get you all over the Oakland Bay Bridge and then side roads to the Berkley Hills. There's an anti-Antifa resistance in Berkeley that's pretty strong. You should be fairly safe if we can get you there. You can rest the wounded girl there for a few days and then the resistance can get you to Richmond. At Richmond, there is a WWII landing craft that's all reconditioned, which will take you and all the soldiers to Sausalito.

Ranger was from Richmond and knew a lot of the people there and assured the group that Richmond wouldn't fall to Antifa.

Max told Ranger that it sounded like a good plan. Ranger said that he would be sending an additional fifty soldiers and that would require two more personnel carriers. He wanted Antifa out of Northern California by next year. The soldiers were going to be stationed in Sausalito to secure the Golden Gate Bridge. He wanted Max to assist and advise Captain Bradley in setting up a position to guard the bridge and the city of Sausalito. The plan was to clean up San Francisco and then move troops across the Golden Gate Bridge and take back Northern California completely.

Max met with Myra and Peng and told them the plan. He instructed them to tell nobody what the plan was, including Ron, concerning Sausalito.

He also told Myra to talk to people at the hospital to obtain contacts for supplies.

Peng spent considerable time with the wounded girl. She found out the girl's name was Quyen and that she had come to the U.S. ten years ago with her parents. They had both died of the plague.

The doctor informed Peng that Quyen had a painful, sexually transmitted disease. He said that he had given her a powerful antibiotic injection and would like Peng to make sure she takes one of these 'vitamin' pills every day for a month. Peng assured the doctor this would be done.

Quyen soon started speaking English again. Peng watched her closely and noticed little things that Quyen was doing which seemed to indicate that she was planning an escape. The skin around her leg bands was raw!

Peng talked with Quyen frequently. Little by little, a bond was developing. Quyen told her, in one of their conversations, that she would try to kill any man that touched her in the wrong way again. Tears welled up in her eyes as she told this to Peng. Peng offered Quyen a job working with her and Myra. Quyen turned this down and said she wanted to work for Max! Peng immediately told her that Max was very experienced and very strong and that she wouldn't be able to do the things that he did. Without pausing, Quyen said, "bullshit" in Mandarin. Peng gave her a strong look and changed the topic.

Ranger contacted Max telling him that they had to leave now. There was a large Antifa group heading towards Oakland. Make sure your people are downstairs and ready to go in thirty minutes. Apparently Antifa was losing ground across the United States and were all retreating to California. He concluded that Antifa is now looking to break off California from the rest of the United States and form a separate country!

It became a madhouse for everyone getting ready in this short period of time. Note that they had to get new clothes on Quyen and put on new bandages. The only clothes available were a small Army uniform. She did not complain.

Ranger emphasized to Max that he wanted Captain Bradley in the same transport with him. Also, that the Captain had little experience but was a good listener and you can bark at him and he won't shut you off. He is from West Point and is trained to understand war. Also, the Air Force can't help us; the president will not use air power on Americans! In conclusion, he shocked Max by telling him that the majority of his soldiers had not been through basic training. The plague had taken its toll!

Ranger also let Max know that his help was greatly appreciated. This lifted Max's spirits. However, Max remembered a time in Afghanistan when he was put on a pedestal and shortly afterwards, he was knocked right off of it. Maybe this was why the Ranger never referred to himself as General.

They left the hospital at the exact time Ranger had planned. Just before they left though, Max observed Ranger 'dress down' a couple of his young, partially trained soldiers that only arrived just in time. He explained that when he said seven a.m., it means 6:45! During this 'dressing down', Ranger's face was no more than one inch from theirs. Ranger did not go along on this mission. He had the entire state of California to take care of and if he died on this dangerous mission along with the Captain and Max, it could be a disastrous outcome for the state.

On the way to the Oakland Bay Bridge, occasional bullets would pelt the personnel carriers. Max wondered if the soldiers that had been dressed down were more afraid of Ranger or the bullets hitting the personnel carrier. He guessed that the incident would be told and retold countless times over beers in the years to come, especially to their children. He was sure that every time the story was told, Ranger would get a bit bigger and meaner!

Max later could not recollect the exact road, street or homeowner's yard they all went through to make it to the Berkeley Hills. After a few miles in the hills, the Captain found a good defensible position and brought the convoy to a stop. His soldiers were quickly dispatched to defensible positions. It was an interesting location. They were about a quarter of a mile from the tree line. The area near the tree line was a large circular area full of nice green grass. It was slightly depressed from the meadow around them. In the rainy season it would fill with water. An old farm road ran thru the tree area to the city of Berkeley. The road was old and not in use. A sign at the Berkeley end of it indicated you should not enter. Max was told of this road and used it to hopefully entrap the Antifa following them. The road was overgrown in many areas.

Upon opening the rear door of the personnel carrier containing the women, the smell of regurgitated breakfast was in the air. Quyen actually appeared in the best condition even though she was still recovering from the gunshot wound. She was the only one that didn't toss her breakfast.

Max was hard at work showing Captain Bradley how the defensive positions worked and where they should be located when Quyen grabbed his arm. She wanted to know where her rifle was and where she should go. Max was entirely dumbfounded. He told the Captain to give him a minute while he attended to an urgent matter.

Captain Bradley saw the situation at hand and a grin appeared on his face. He had heard the story about Quyen and to see her wearing the Army uniform touched his heart too. He wished he could change these Antifa people instead of killing them.

Max took Quyen to the personnel carrier and gave her the smallest rifle he could find. With her wound, she did not need to lug around a heavy weapon. The rifle was a WW II M-1 carbine with a couple extra clips and box of bullets. He showed the rifle to Quyen and that the safety was on and how to put in a clip. He also told her not to take the safety off until he gave her permission. He also gave her a pair of binoculars and showed her how to focus them. He then gave her an order to stay within ten feet of Captain Bradley at all times. Her job would be to protect him from snipers. Max explained that snipers usually look for the highest-ranking officer to shoot and her job was to try to prevent Captain Bradley from getting shot. Quyen felt the job sounded extremely important and God forbid anyone taking aim at the Captain!

The Captain finally gave the order to stop and eat. It was four in the afternoon and no one had eaten since breakfast. Quyen kept within ten feet of the Captain, she did not walk over to eat. Max saw her still on guard and told her to sit down and eat and then relax before she opens her wound up. She replied that she wasn't hungry and her wound was not bleeding any more. She asked if she could bring some sandwiches to the two soldiers visible at the tree line to the left. She went on to say it was down hill all the way and she would take it real slow. Max said okay, because he had not received any messages from the scouts on any enemy activity. He emphasized again to take it slow and find out what those two soldiers were hearing, if anything, and call me on the field phone.

Quyen grabbed a few sandwiches, a bottle of water, her rifle, and headed out to the two soldiers. When she arrived, she found the PFC with the dark hair, Larry, asleep! The PFC with the light brown hair, Gregg, did not hear her arrive. She alerted them of her presence by throwing the bag of sandwiches at their feet. She said, "I could have killed you both." Gregg, in turn, told her to get her skinny little ass back up to the top of the hill! With that reply, Quyen stomped on their sandwiches. In unison, Larry and Gregg called her a bitch. Just when Quyen was about to respond, bullets slammed into the branches above them. Quyen quickly dropped to the ground and took aim at the two soldiers in black running at them. She dropped them before they even took aim at her.

Quyen, in her oversized uniform and tennis shoes, clearly took charge. She yelled at them to stop firing until they saw something. They could hear a lot of gunfire in the distance now, but not yet close to them. She picked up the field phone and called the command center at the personnel carriers. Max answered and a very excited Quyen informed him that they had contact with the enemy and had put two of them down. She went on to tell him that they could hear gunfire towards Berkeley. And she could tell from the gunshots that there was shotguns being used by some of them. It was her impression that Antifa were being pushed towards their position. She told Max that she was scared and her back hurts. She also said that Larry and Gregg do not know I am scared; I don't want them to run and leave me!

Max assured her that they wouldn't run, explaining that they didn't run when Ranger dressed them down. He told her to listen up, and said, "Corporal", you're in charge! I want you three to hide. It is too dangerous to run up the hill where we are. You would be shot in the back. Get under a log, some dirt, up a tree, whatever, I don't want them to see you three. What I can put together from the reports I've got from the scouts, is that there are five hundred or so Antifa running as fast as they can from an unidentified enemy. They are most likely scared, especially on this dark night. This can easily happen with inexperienced soldiers. I want them out in the open!

Max immediately reviewed the plans with Captain Bradley. The Captain agreed but worried that there may be too many Antifa soldiers. Max countered that they had a lot of firepower with the women armed with automatic weapons. From Max's point of view, his women wouldn't even have to be good shooters; it would be like shooting into a bowl.

Captain Bradley called all his positions and scouts to get ready and not to shoot too soon. If shots were fired too soon, Antifa soldiers could retreat and that could get quite messy for the Berkeley volunteers. Each woman was given an automatic rifle and the Captain set up a fifty-caliber machine gun on a tripod and planned to operate it himself. Max did not assign himself a position; if anything below got out hand he would do what he could to fix it. He knew that they had to keep them in the fish bowl below and not let them advance up the hill. There was nothing he could do for the three below. Only Max had experienced this type of action before. Everyone knew what had to be done.

It did not take long until the Antifa soldiers started emerging into the open field below the hill. The darkness hid the personnel carriers on the top of the hill. With night vision glasses, Max watched them as they came out of the woods. He also tried to find Quyen, Larry and Gregg. He thought he saw someone in a tree and maybe the butt of a rifle protruding from a bush.

Soon, the majority of the five hundred Antifa troops were out of the woods when someone fired a shot! Someone in the rear of the Antifa soldiers yelled, "It's a trap!" As best Max could tell, the enemy was taking fire from the right side. This could have confused a possible retreat. There was also a lot of gunfire to the rear. It had to be from their scouts and the Berkeley volunteers.

Max had the personnel carriers pointed down the hill and turned the lights on them. Max, Captain Bradley, and the women fired clip after clip into the bowl. The Captains 50 was almost red hot. It was a total massacre for the Antifa forces. The shooting continued until there was no movement. The remaining Berkeley Volunteers emerged form the woods and were amazed at all the dead they saw.

Myra was one of the first to reach the carnage, looking for wounded. She and Peng found Quyen, Larry and Gregg! It did not take long to pronounce all three dead. Peng took a number of pictures of the three.

Myra noticed the leader of the Berkeley Volunteers was wounded in the arm leg and chest and didn't even know it! It took considerable effort to get him on to the stretcher and to the personnel carrier, where there was light.

Max counted and checked the Antifa soldiers to make sure there was nobody left in this mess who was alive and could still operate a gun. Of the five hundred Antifa soldiers, Max only found five of them alive. They all died soon after he found them. On a different day, they may have been spared, but Max had just seen his Corporal and two PFC's lying dead next to each other. Max had seen death many times before but this got to him. He did not cry, but tears ran from his eyes. Myra came running when she saw Max's tears but then she saw the three dead again and he had to hold her up.

Myra checked and officially pronounced that seven of the Berkeley Volunteers as dead. She and Peng then went to work on the remaining wounded. Help from the city of Berkeley arrived in a couple hours to pick up the wounded and the dead. The Army dead and the Berkeley Volunteers dead were brought to a mortuary in Berkeley. The people of Berkeley wanted to have the Volunteers and the Army dead buried in a monument area where they had died in the battle. All parties consented. Quyen would be buried as an Army Corporal.

Max worked it out with the mortician that two Army soldiers in the day and two during the night would be guarding the caskets until they were buried. Also, the caskets of Gregg, Larry and Quyen would be buried next to each other, the same as a picture he handed the mortician. The mortician was troubled by the picture and had to pause for a minute. Peng was given the task of researching Quyen's life, in order to locate her relatives in China.

After checking with his people, Ranger told Max that it was safe to drive to Sausalito with the personnel carriers. After this major loss for Antifa in the Battle of Berkeley Hills, the Antifa soldiers in Northern California disappeared.

The economy in the U.S. was improving day by day. California's economy trailed in the nation due to Antifa's high presence there. However, improvements were showing. The newspapers were printing again and a few TV stations were back on the air. A full-page picture of Gregg, Larry and Quyen all lying dead together was on the front page of all the newspapers. It appeared from the picture that Gregg and Larry died while trying to shield Quyen. They did not know if that was how it all went down, but the press went with it and some of the papers had to put out a second and third edition!

There were definite signs that the press and most of the people were no longer on the side of the globalists and now there was activity to make Max the President of a new nation called California. This movement was unexpected for the national government. Also, posters for Max, as president were appearing everywhere. In fact, on the day of the burial of the Army's and Volunteers dead at the Battle of Berkeley monument, Max was the featured speaker.

Much later, Myra saw Max looking at the picture of Gregg, Larry ad Quyen lying dead on the ground. She heard him say, "and those two boys did not run", and slammed his hand on the table. Myra quietly backed out of the room.

Max always vehemently denied his importance in the Battle of Berkeley Hills. He always gave credit to the soldiers and the Berkeley Volunteers that held the line. But it didn't matter how many times he said it, the people and the press always made Max the hero.

Chapter 10

Exiled

Ranger contacted Max and wanted to meet him on the Golden Gate Bridge, immediately. Max did not ask why, he spent his working years in the military and if someone higher in rank gave you an order, you did it.

It was cool and misty in the late morning when they met on the bridge. After greeting formalities Ranger informed Max that his marina, boat, and car were most likely bugged and that is why we are meeting here.

The mist was increasing and they walked downwind so they could hear each other better. Ranger, who had become a close personal friend to Max, said he had a source in the CIA that told him they were going to look the other way when the globalists try to take Max out. In short, they saw Max as a liability, now that Antifa was all but eliminated. They were afraid the people of California would get Max to be the President/Governor of California. They fear the people will follow you and the United States can't allow a state to secede from the Union. If the globalists fail, the CIA will do the job, he said to Max.

Every day there seemed to be a new article on the Battle of Berkeley Hills. The latest contained maps of the battle, illustrating how the scouts arrived just in time to push the Antifa forces into the fish bowl. It went on to say that the scouts received orders from Max to support the Berkeley Volunteers, of which many, by the time the scouts got there, were wounded, dead or exhausted. These scouts ran approximately two miles to reach the Berkeley Volunteers. They had run straight into the group trying to retreat. Hand to hand combat ensued, forcing the remaining enemy into the fish bowl. All three scouts, it reported, had died, along with seven of the Berkeley Volunteers.

Yet, on another day, an article came out on the Battle of Berkeley Hills that depicted how the women at the personnel carriers had turned the vehicles around to shine lights on the enemy and raining three thousand rounds on the enemy below, actually won the day. There was much debate on the details as to how everything all went down and how precisely the battle was won.

Max stopped walking and stared out into the bay. Nothing was said for about five minutes. Finally, Max's thought process put it all together. He remembered that he thought someone was following him yesterday. He knew they would keep sending assassins until one of them got lucky. They might even go after Myra to draw him out.

He turned and confronted Ranger and told him that he and Myra would be gone before sunset. He was going to tell Ranger where they were going but Ranger spoke first," Do not tell anyone where you are going."

They quietly walked back to the marina. Ranger saw Myra and gave her an almost emotional hug and left. Myra saw something in the Ranger's eyes and felt something in the hug that confused her. She turned to look at Max and saw even more disturbing signs.

Max told Myra to get in the Jeep because he wanted to take a walk with her in Muir Woods. Myra loved that place and didn't argue about going. Sometimes, to Ron's dismay, they would go there on Sunday instead of church. Max had told her once that Muir Woods put him closer to his maker that church!

On their drive to Muir Woods, Max did not say anything. That was okay with Myra, because she was busy trying to figure out the significance of Ranger's hug and the seriousness in Max's face. She was also wondering why the .45 was stuck in his belt.

They turned into the park and then into the parking lot. There were a few cars. Tourism had not come back yet since the plague. Max noticed a black pickup followed him into the parking lot and parked near his Jeep.

Aft the huge Sequoias surrounded them, Max told Myra about the meeting he had with Ranger. He spared none of the details and added a few that the Ranger was too kind to tell him. Myra was quick to understand. They agreed that they would take the sailboat and once they got a hundred miles off the coast, they would discuss where to go. It was also agreed that Myra would go for a walk with Peng and tell her that they would be gone for maybe three years. Only few details would be given.

Suddenly, an armed assassin came out from behind the tree next to them. The assassin instructed them in broken English, to walk down towards the stream. Max would have none of that and turned to confront him. The assassin's gun jammed. Myra was directly behind Max and she grabbed the .45. Now the assassin was looking down the barrel of a gun. Max grabbed the man's arm and twisted it behind his back. He told Myra to take the man's gun. Then he smelled arsenic and the assassin fell to the ground.

The corpse had a strange look to him. His mouth was still open from trying to gasp for his last breath. Myra could see an extra row of teeth in his mouth. They checked his clothes and found no identification. Myra pulled out her cell phone and took pictures of the corpse. Max picked up the assassin's gun and noticed that it was a Luger. They left the corpse on the ground. It smelled of evil and neither one of them wanted to touch it. They headed back to the Jeep. They were both scared and at a loss for words.

As soon as they got back to the marina, Myra went to find Peng. She told Peng what her and Max were going to do and why. Peng said it was a lot to grasp but that she understood. Peng then surprised Myra. She said that Andrew was getting very involved with a slut and she was worried that he was going to get hurt. I know this little slut is trying to get pregnant! I want you to talk with him and take him along on your trip. I will lie and tell him it's a short trip. He believes all the sluts lies so why shouldn't he believe mine? Peng looked very bitter.

Andrew was told of the trip and was anxious to go. He got his clothes together and put them in a pillowcase. Max had told him that he could not take his cell phone along because they could be tracked with it. He had always obeyed Max and Max trusted him. Max also thought that there might be another side to this slut story.

Chapter 11

Sailing to South America

Max and Myra said their goodbyes to everybody. Max and Ron actually prayed together and Max appeared serious. That corpse had scared the hell out of him!

Max headed to the boat with a lot of money on him. A lot of it came from dead people that died of the plague. It was not something that he was proud of, but the money was doing nobody any good where it was.

Max had been working on his boat for some time. When Antifa was burning and attacking boats on the bay and on the ocean, he decided to fortify certain areas to give protection from bullets. He had also kept it well stocked with water, fuel, spare parts, and non-perishable food. Max was anxious to take off while the tide was going out.

Someone yelled to Max as he was working with some of the gear on the boat. It was Fred, hero of the marina battle. He wanted to know what the hell was going on. Well, considering it was Fred, who had saved his bacon at the marina battle, Max decided to confide in him. Fred said that he had nothing to do and that he had been to South America many times and had even married a girl from over there once. "You could use a man like me," Fred said, and then after a short pause, "I've got three cases of PBR sitting at the house."

Max was stuck now. Fred could be deadweight; on the other hand, do you know how hard it must have been to buy PBR in San Francisco? People in this part of the country tended to want an umbrella in their drink. "OK, Fred, you're on the team. We leave in half an hour".

In half an hour everyone was on board and they were off. They had not kept their secret of leaving Sausalito very well and it was worrying Max. After about five miles, Max saw a boat following them. Soon they were crossing under the Golden Gate Bridge, which always reminded him of his dad going under the same bridge in an old World War II Liberty Ship (troop ship) on his way to Vietnam. His dad's description of it sounded about the same as Max was seeing it now. The top part was shrouded in fog. Max got emotional every time he passed under that bridge. This time he was apprehensive though, like his father must have been, because real danger was most likely ahead of them.

Andrew was doing the sailing. Max's experience with sailing was not on the same level as Andrew's. Max had mostly just sailed around the bay. Max instructed Andrew to go about fifty miles west and then turn to the north.

Myra and Fred were still working on getting everything organized and tied down. Every ten minutes or so, Max would pick up the binoculars to see if that boat was still following them. Andrew asked Max why they should turn north and Max told him that it was because he was pretty sure that they were being followed! Max saw that they were getting closer every time he checked. It was not a sailboat, which meant that they would have to turn around at some point to get more fuel. A sailboat is much slower than a motorboat and Max was worried that they could catch up and try to do them harm.

The sun was almost set now and a cloudbank was approaching from the north. The wind was also picking up, which concerned Andrew because he had little experience in heavy seas. It must have also concerned the people on the motorboat because they turned around.

Max told Andrew to take down the sails and put up the storm jib, then they would all sit down, make some sandwiches and make some plans. Once they all sat down and had a sandwich in their hands, the conversation began. Myra thought they should head up north and find an island in the Aleutian chain where they could set up a camp. Max liked the idea in the short term but was worried because the people in the motorboat had seen them turn north. Fred did not make a comment, he was not sure if he was an equal member of the group.

Andrew then surprised everybody by showing half a dozen or so pages on sightings of Soros and Hitler, picked up from the radio station he was always listening to. He noted that a number of these sightings were in South America. Also, the latest on the location of the first incident of the plague occurring was in the Amazon. There was a conspiracy theory that there was a headquarters somewhere in the Andes or the Amazon.

Fred was scratching his head now. Finally, he decided to tell the group that he had been to Argentina and Chile, which might be helpful. He admitted that he had a bias against going north, the cold made his joints hurt.

There was some more quiet time and then Max told the group that he wasn't one for conspiracy theories but he couldn't help but think about the fact that he had found a map on the assassin that had attacked him and Myra in Muir Woods. It wasn't much of a map and he hadn't even bothered to show it to Myra. He still had it in his wallet though. Max retrieved the small, oily piece of paper and they all gathered around to look at it. There was a word on there and then an arrow or line going to a small river that started in some mountains and flowed east. Max could not make out the word. Fred thought it looked German and he looked more closely. "Conception, but I'm just guessing."

Nobody had heard of that city or place before. Andrew got out his computer and found many Conceptions. The one he found most interesting was in Chile. Now everyone was gathered around the computer. Max said," That's interesting, note that Chile and Argentina border each other."

With the storm jib working well, Andrew stayed topside with the weather gear on while everyone else stayed below and retired for the night. About an hour later, Fred joined Andrew. He felt that no one should be alone at night, especially in a storm.

The storm turned out to be stronger than anticipated. Even with the rain gear on, Fred and Andrew were soon drenched to the bone. Around 4 am, Max brought them some coffee. After an assessment of their location, they figured that the storm had blown them south about twenty miles during the night. They changed course with an intention of getting about twenty miles form shore. The wind was still strong. They couldn't put up the mainsail because winds like these could easily rip it. They kept the storm jib up and let the storm do its thing.

After reviewing the maps, a conclusion was reached that it would take around twenty days to sail to Conception. They all took turns being topside. Andrew spent his spare time looking at a map of the city of Conception. He could not find a road that would lead to the stream they would need to follow.

Andrew studied the city of Conception. There were approximately 300,000 people living there. Also, there were several marinas and one with a covered storage facility. In addition, there was a four-star hotel. It was too soon to determine where to stay, what to do with the boat, should they buy a Jeep, etc. He made copies of all the material on the area that he could find and gave them to the rest of the group.

The storm did not let up. Myra made soup for everyone. Max found a minor leak in the boat and immediately fixed it. Andrew slept all afternoon. Myra and Max put on wet gear and monitored the actions of the boat. The storm jib was in control. Although they had a window in the cockpit and a canvas roof, a blast of ocean water from the rear or the side would still get them wet.

The intensity of the storm was increasing. They couldn't manage to tune in to any weather station. They were all okay, and the equipment was functioning fine. However, Fred and Myra were seasick, but they were both feeling much better by morning. It was still overcast the next morning.

Finally, around noon on the eighth day, the satellite told them that they were about four hundred miles north of Hawaii! They used all available information and set a course for Lima, Peru. The weather wasn't ugly anymore and the sailing was beautiful. The temperature was in the 60s.

Fred attempted to do some fishing. Max sat down beside him and offered him a PBR. He could tell Fred was happy and was beginning to feel like part of the group.

Later on Max was adjusting the light in his bedroom and something from the ceiling dropped to the floor. It was a tracking device that was sending a signal of their position. He showed everyone and they were all shocked. He threw it into the ocean. It may have been a blessing in disguise. It had been showing them as being on a course for Hawaii. Max had everyone scour the boat. No other device was found. Max knew that if the person who planted the device was professional, they would find a place that you would never think to look.

The weather was considerably warmer in these latitudes. They were all getting a little sunburned. The food supply was ample but most of it was from the survival food containers. They were all thrilled that Fred turned out to be a great fisherman. The evening meal now was generally a fish steak of some sort that he had caught. It usually required a full can of sterno to get the fish cooked. A love for sushi at this point would have saved them many cans, but nobody was having that. Andrew tried to catch a fish every day too. Fred taught him a lot on how to fish, but he did not have the luck Fred had.

The moon was full, making for some beautiful night sailing. However, due too very little wind, they made little progress. Using the motor was pondered but there was a fear that if they needed the fuel in an emergency, they would be out of luck. Max explained that he had brought along five extra cans of diesel fuel. He felt comfortable with using up to twenty gallons to get them on their way. He added that the wind generator was not charging the batteries and the ocean water desalinates on electricity. The meals they were cooking with the sterno were using up almost the entire supply as well. Everyone agreed to use the motor again.

Myra was starting to go stir crazy. To keep her sanity, she decided to go to her cabin and write the great American novel. Her first chapter told of how her and Max had met in Omaha. Eventually she came to her nursing career and Dr. Thorpe. At that point, she started feeling miserable and dirty. She had sold her soul to get what she wanted!

Myra never did take confession with Reverend Ron, as Max had wanted her to. Writing about the past caused her to hate herself again. About that time, Max walked in to the room and saw Myra with her head under the pillow. He jokingly asked her whom she was hiding from and instantly regretted it. Myra was never fond of Max's humor. Max knew what she was crying about. He remembered when Myra wanted him to beat her. It was something he could not do! Myra thought that if only Max would have beaten her, she would feel better today.

After Myra stopped crying, Max suggested they see a doctor in Conception and find out if the procedure the doctor used on her could be reversed. Myra had heard that it could be reversed, but that was in the

United States, not a third world country. She also informed Max that she was doing very well with her new book until she got to the part about the plague and Dr. Thorpe! She did not want to have a conversation about Dr. Thorpe so she told Max that she needed to get some rest. Max patted her lovingly on the shoulder and then went topside.

Fred happened to be resting in his cabin during Myra and Max's conversation. He had heard it all. He wanted to help Myra but knew it was not a good idea and she would know he had eavesdropped on their entire conversation. So, he waited until it was Myra's turn at the helm, when no one else was around.

After some small talk, a couple of days later, Fred told Myra that he needed to talk to someone and get something off his chest. Myra asked him if he could talk to her, or was it a guy thing? Fred laughed about it being a guy thing and then in a more solemn tone, he told her that he wanted to talk about the battle at the marina. Fred told her not to tell anyone and then told her about how he had received much praise for his part in the battle and may have been a key player. He said that when the Antifa soldiers walked past his house on their way to the marina, he had just hung up the phone on his fourth wife. She had just told him that she was leaving him for someone else! He had heard the shooting at the marina and grabbed his 12-gauge pump shotgun and walked right down the center of the street, hoping to be killed. But he wasn't even wounded! Every time one of them had turned to shoot on Fred, they exposed themselves too Max's keen eye. Max had killed most of them and Fred didn't even get a scratch! I could never have been the hero without walking down the center of that street, hoping to die!

Fred concluded by saying that he does no think of his ex-wives anymore. He was just happy to be an important player with his new friends. He no longer wanted to live in the past. Tears were coming out of Fred's eyes and he could not let Myra see that. He told her he'd better leave now.

They quickly used up the twenty gallons of fuel they had planned on using. The batteries were charged up again and there was now a surplus of desalinated water at the end of the day. The days were getting cooler, just like fall in Sausalito. It was apparent that everyone was thinking about Sausalito now. They all hoped that they would be able to return some day.

Andrew was a little homesick for his mother, brother and dad. He was also homesick for the relationship he had with his girlfriend. He hoped that she had stopped taking those pills. He was worried that if his mother caught her when she was high, she would get ahold of her good! He was also afraid of her seeing other guys. The thought of that really disgusted him. Andrew had always had bad luck with girls. Sometimes it was hard for him to fall asleep because he was plagued by that notion.

At this point, Fred was just fat and happy. He would navigate the boat for five or six hours then snack a little, nap a little and then try to catch a fish. He could study all the clouds as he fished. The clouds in the south came up further north every day. Fred figured it would not be long until they got some rain. In anticipation of the rain, they collected everything that would hold water. He quickly set the items, buckets, bowls, and glasses, in a safe and strategic location on deck. He also figured out ways to prevent them from blowing away. If it rained that night and everyone was below deck, Fred decided that he would give himself a salt bath, using the bucket and then just standing in the rain to rinse the salt off. Everybody else had bathed this way and little innuendos directed at Fred were getting more frequent. He did not feel that he smelled, so he had been ignoring them. Finally, he yielded to the pressure and the first night it rained, he accomplished the feat. He hoped everyone was happy now. He also threw his clothes away and put on new ones. He figured someone would just complain about the dirty clothes next.

The clouds were certainly getting heavier. There was considerable lightning, which scared everyone on the boat. Myra put on a raincoat; she wanted to be outside when the rain started. Finally, it started. It came down hard and felt very cold. The sea was still calm. They were now making good time. After a while, the winds intensified and the strong gusts followed. Suddenly, the mainsail tore. They quickly dropped it and secured it with ropes.

There was another mainsail below deck but decided not to make an attempt to bring it up and put it on the mast. The storm jib was going to be used until the storm was over. It put a sense of worry in the air that maybe the boat would come apart!

They all lamented on their lack of sailing experience. Sailing had seemed so safe and simple when they were sailing in moderate winds. It didn't put anyone at ease either when Max told everybody to put on a lifejacket.

Myra and Max went below deck and made some tea. Max brought some tea up to Fred and Andrew, who didn't seem to mind the storm.

Myra and Max got caught up in another activity. They found it most cozy to have a blanket over them and listen to the rain pelt the roof of the boat. Even in a storm, they felt safe when they were together. While they were alone, Max revealed his tentative plan on what they should do when they got to Conception, which may take a year or so. He thought Andrew should take a course on Spanish at the college in the city. He felt that if Andrew started off with just one course, the college might not ask for a high school graduation certificate. Myra felt that Fred should take the course too. Supposedly, Fred already knew some Spanish, mostly words like 'Cervesa'. Max had seen something on the computer about how there were tourist excursions into the mountains. He felt that would be a good way to get to know the areas on the map he had found on the assassin. Max concluded that they must always have at least one person on the boat while docked, until they felt they could trust the people.

They were all getting anxious to get to Conception. Without exception, they all felt that sailboats travel very slowly! Myra continued on with writing her novel. She felt more comfortable with herself and the troubling things from her past after talking to Fred. She now looked at Fred as a father figure and began to see life more the way he did.

Andrew, excitedly, came to Max saying he did hours of research on the Lugar that Max had taken off of the assassin that had tried to kill Max and Myra back in Muir Woods. He said he found a source on Google that gave information on the serial number on the pistol. The source said it was the property of the Third Reich and was manufactured in 1939 in Dusseldorf, Germany.

Andrew went on to say that he was very careful not to touch the gun with his bare hands. He was hoping to find an expert in Conception who could lift the fingerprints off of it. Max told Andrew that he'd done good work. He added though, that it would be a long shot to get a fingerprint from it. He added that it would be very hard to find a match to someone in Germany or wherever. If they did get a fingerprint, Max thought that Ranger might be of some help. He had once told Max he had connections in Interpol. He thought it was a very outside chance. This was all starting to get interesting.

The rains finally stopped. They met a cruise ship they supposed was heading for Hawaii. This was encouraging to everyone because it indicated the world economy was improving.

Andrew figured that they were three days from Conception. The sky was clear and they had good wind form the west. The food supply was getting dangerously low. Everyone was ready to fire Fred as the fisherman. Fred was not concerned; he knew there would be fish near the coast.

Max was moving the mainsail from the storage area and exposed his two cases of PBR! He was totally shocked. With all the excitement, he had plum forgot about it. Fred quipped that Max not finding the PBR until now indicated that he was not an alcoholic. Fred devised a crate to put six beers in to drag in the water for about half an hour to get them cold. He also, along with Andrew, put extra effort into their fishing and it did finally bring results. They caught two beautiful white-sea bass. One of those critters weighed forty pounds!

Max carved it up and put it on the grill he had mounted on the rear of the boat when they were in Sausalito. The heating source was one of their last few cans of sterno.

Everyone was allotted two PBR's. There was a question as to whether or not Myra should get two because of her size and her degrading comments about beer drinkers. The males quickly lost the argument, partially because Max stayed out of it. White-sea bass with PBR was perfect.

The wind subsided so the four of them went to work on the replacing of the mainsail. None of the four amateur sailors had ever done this before. Andrew leaned over to far at one point and fell into the drink. This created quite a commotion because they had to turn the boat around. Also, they discovered there are no brakes on a sailboat. Everyone had a good laugh at Andrew's expense.

Eventually, they did get the mainsail properly attached and everyone learned some new words from Fred. It was a red sail that did not match the other sails, but there were no complaints.

Tomorrow they would see the city of Conception. Myra was on sailing duty until midnight. Max planned to keep her company. The sun was about to set and Andrew and Fred were teasing the fish with some homemade lures. Suddenly, without warning, a whale bumped the boat. Fred and Andrew looked straight into the whale's eyes. There was no damage done.

It was decided that the whale was just saying hello. It was also decided that this was a good omen. Andrew said, "Praise be to God." He said he felt his dad would have wanted him to say that!

In the morning they still could not see the city of Conception. Andrew handed out twenty or so copies of sites to see in the city. The pictures made the city out to be very large. They all felt it would take a long time to get to know the city. They did not see any boat slips in any of the pictures. Where to dock the boat could turn out to be a big problem. Later on, Andrew continued to look for a radio station that was broadcasting in English. Eventually he found one. After about fifteen minutes, the station came to the news segment. To his shock, they reported that the city had gone back under martial law. They had another name for it but it was essentially the same thing. The main problem causing this setback was their inability to get their economy moving again since the plague. Over fifty percent of the people were unemployed and this was causing riots. Food was now in short supply.

After hearing this, Andrew called for an urgent meeting. Andrew reviewed what he had just heard on the radio. He stated that it would not be safe to go there. They need a new plan. There was a pause while everyone digested this new information. He also said that he had been skeptical for a while now of the map that had been taken off of the assassin. Maybe he needed to do more research on the map, he thought. It could turn out that we were interpreting the map wrong. Sailing certainly gave a person a lot of time to think. They decided to set a course for Lima.

Max told Andrew to keep researching it. They needed to know where the first incident of the plague had occurred. Max wanted to go there. Myra reminded everyone that they were not on any kind of deadline. And you might say that this is a make work vacation project to stay away from Sausalito for Max's safety for a while. Fred had nothing to say except that he agreed. They all agreed to sail on, sail on and sail on. Fred was doing more of the sailing now. He kept the boat within approximately twenty miles of the coast. Everyone was safe while he was at the wheel. He always paid attention to what he was doing. Myra went back to her novel and also to help out with the food. Andrew continued to do what he liked best, researching the conspiracy theory. It was obvious that he already believed it. There were multiple theories. First, Soros and a lot of the very rich elites had taken the red pill. Second, that certain Nazis from WWII were hiding out somewhere taking the red pill also. They all wanted globalism/to rule the world!

Max was the first to complain about living on a diet of fish. The others occasionally made comments also. Max told Andrew to check out Valparaiso on the computer to find out if supplies could be obtained there. Also, to look for a hotel that was near a marina.

Andrew was all over this project. He found that Valparaiso was called the cultural capital of the country. It was also syncopated, dilapidated, colorful and poetic. He always relayed to everyone when he found something of interest.

They were making good time on their way to Valparaiso. The wind and the water current were with them. The idea that this city was known as the 'little San Francisco' got everyone excited.

Fred kept observing the mountains in the distance getting taller. Some of them now had snow on their peaks. This was interesting to Fred because they were getting closer to the equator. The way Fred saw it, they would be in Valparaiso by noon the next day.

Max came over to join Fred and share a PBR with him. He told Fred that he considered him to be one of his best friends. They rehashed the battle at the marina again. And once again, he told Fred that he had more courage than anyone he had ever known. He was amazed that Fred had walked down the middle of the street like that.

They also talked about Quyen. "You know," Fred said, "those three died together. There must be some solace in dying together. I unquestionably believe all three were really, really close in the end. I think if any one of them wanted to run, they would have. There was nothing to stop them from running!"

Myra came up topside and observed two grown men crying. She yelled to them, acting like she did not see anything. "Are you guys ready for another beer?" Myra did not want any part of that conversation; the bodies of those three were still warm when she checked them on the ground. It was one of the hardest things she had ever encountered.

Myra came back with more beer and changed the subject. It was a beautiful evening. They observed about fifteen minutes of flying fish. None of them had ever seen flying fish before. One of them landed on the rear of the deck. Max had to grab it and throw it back in the ocean.

Both Myra and Fred noticed there was a boat following them. They figured the boat was about a mile away. They all looked again and couldn't see anything. It had turned its lights off. Max felt it was not normal for a captain to turn of the lights like that. He got the binoculars out and saw that they were doing the same. It was a motorboat and had no business being in these waters.

Myra went below and retrieved the .45 and the M-14. She dragged them across the deck so the people on the motorboat could not see them. The game plan was to not let on that they had guns and hopefully the motorboat would swing wide of the dumb sailboat people and they would never see them again.

The motorboat kept coming right towards them, so Max went on a different plan. Max, looking through the binoculars, noticed that there was at least one rifle on the motorboat. Max's original thought was that they either have no guns or many guns. He was becoming more concerned. There was no indication that it was a police boat. Also, it was a powerboat with twin engines.

Max knew that if he could hit those outboard motors with the M-14, he could shut them down. Hopefully they were on the assumption that the sailboat had no guns.

The motorboat started rapidly gaining now. Max had Fred stand in the reinforced stairwell for protection. He also kept his rifle out of sight. Max laid his .45 on the instrument panel.

The motorboat was about half a mile away now. Max could hit that boat well at this range, but was there another reason they were running without lights? This was becoming dangerous business. He thought about using a show of force, having everyone topside with guns in their hands. That could be dangerous business too, he thought. He decided to switch guns with Fred. He yelled to Fred to switch guns with him. Fred brought him the M-14. Max then told him to tell Andrew to get a flare gun and to fire it from the port window when he yells. He also mentioned to be careful not to hit the other boat with the flare, unless the shooting starts, of course. He also sent for Myra to come up with a couple of those Barrettas, adding that he was feeling lonely up there.

When Max yelled, Andrew fired a flare up and over the motorboat from the port window. It was something unexpected by the people on the motorboat. They went right on by and waved. They shall never know if the people on that boat had evil intentions. However, they did turn their lights on after they passed.

Everyone gave a sigh of relief. Max said that they would have won the fight and sunk their boat, but they could have suffered casualties too. Once again, Andrew said, "Praise be to God." It took awhile for everyone to calm down.

It was now late at night. No one could sleep after all the excitement. Myra put a pot of coffee on. She noticed that this was the last of their coffee. She thought it would be nice if she and Max could sleep in a hotel the next night.

Max figured that now was a good time to do some planning. Everyone was wide-awake with a cup of coffee in there hand. He told the group that they could stay in Valparaiso for three or four days if they could find a suitable place to dock the boat and also find a halfway decent hotel to stay in. He wanted someone on or near the boat at all times. He noted though that at Lima, they would have to find a place to leave the boat for an extended period of time if they wanted to go up through the mountains and take a boat down the Amazon. He also noted that if they all went to the Amazon, they would have to figure out where on the boat to hide the guns and how to secure the boat. We have some obstacles to contend with, but I'm sure we can figure it out.

They all noticed that Myra had fallen asleep. Max picked the poor thing up, told Fred that he was in charge of sailing. Max took Myra to bed and noted how confronting a possible enemy with a gun drained every one's energy.

Myra and Max slept late. They were slow about getting ready. Max noticed, as Myra was getting ready, that she had gained a few pounds. He figured that living on a boat could do that. He decided not to bring it to her attention, which was easily the best decision he would make all day!

Finally, around 9 o'clock, they made it topside. It was cool and a jacket was required. In the distance, they could see Valparaiso.

Andrew had the sailing route marked out on a map on the table. Everyone hoped things would work out well and that they would be walking on dry land yet that day.

Max and Fred discussed what had happened the previous night. Neither of them saw a name or identification number or even a flag on the boat. They decided to keep an eye out for the boat in the marina areas in Valparaiso. They both wanted a cup of coffee but there wasn't any!

Max was day tripping with the idea of spreading a rumor that he wanted to get ahold of some red pills. It was one of those fleeting ideas that float through your brain. The general theory out there was that the red pill was made from the ingredients of a plant that grew deep in the Amazon Rain Forest. Max finally concluded that the people of Valparaiso would not be the ones to ask. The people in the Amazon, on the other hand might know something. Max put his red pill thoughts aside and began thinking about things they could do to have fun in Valparaiso.

Later on, in the morning, when they were about an hour away from Valparaiso, Max received a phone call from Ranger. After saying hello etc., Max received an offer of $100,000 to come back and take care of a problem situation in Los Angeles. He was told that most of California had been eradicated of these Antifa crap weasels, however, there was still a nest of them in the Tar Pit area of Los Angeles. They were in a high-rise building near the Tar Pits.

Max had heard about the Tar Pits area and he was very amused by the term 'crap weasel', which was new to him. Ranger said that he had come up with that handle all on his own. Actually, he felt that they should be called something far worse! He had lost quite a few soldiers to those vermin.

Max told him that city fighting was nasty business. However, he had cleaned up a number of messes in cities in Afghanistan. You stand to lose a lot of soldiers, but it can be done. Snipers will be the main problem.

Ranger told Max that he had already lost a lot of men and the gutless Generals were considering making some kind of deal with them. Ranger felt it wasn't the right course of action; he would rather that they be liquidated!

Max agreed and went on to say that it would take him about a month to take care of what he was doing. Just keep your soldiers out of harm's way until I get back. It could be that they will starve to death by then anyway. Also, find the best snipers you can get. I would like to see about fifty snipers located about a block or more from different angles to that building. If they so much as stick a finger out of one of the windows, shoot it off! Also, if you can, land a chopper on top of the building with a team of soldiers. Have them camp out up there. And, if you can, figure out a way to pipe country music on to each floor. Have plenty of fire equipment around in case the crap weasels decide to blow the place.

Ranger said it could be a job-losing situation if they decide to blow up the place. The building contains hundreds of priceless artifacts.

Max asked Ranger if he knew where he was. Ranger informed Max that they have always known exactly where he was. We've had a satellite following you every step of the way. Oh, and that listening device you threw overboard wasn't ours. He paused for a few seconds and then added that one of the screens that monitor your boat has observed Fred relieving himself off the rear of the boat! There are two ladies here who would like to have his cell number. Ranger also expressed deep concern over the boat that had approached them the night before and said they were bad guys!

Chapter 12

Valparaiso

Andrew, Max and Fred worked together navigating the sailboat into the waterway approach to the city. They soon took down the sails and used the engine. There were a number of marina type locations. They finally found a suitable docking on Joliet road. Its location to the inner city was okay.

The people at the marina guaranteed that the boats were very well taken care of. They sold Max, so they were off to a Chilean authentic eatery for lunch. They received well-written instructions on how to get there. It took about an hour, which gave them time to see some sites and listen to the people.

The people at the marina explained that the city was situated on forty-two hills, and on each hill, there were stairs and a rail lift to get to the top of the hill. They were called funiculars. To see all the shops and residences on the hillsides and with each one painted a different color was quite extraordinary. They all liked riding the funiculars. Sometimes there were slides that you could take to get down the hill.

The city was not crowded. On occasion they would see people that looked very sad. And once they saw a man consoling his wife who just started spontaneously crying. They asked a waiter at the restaurant about what they were seeing on the streets and he told them that the plague had wiped out entire families and fortunes. He added that many people would never get over it.

To get everybody in a better mood, the waiter brought everyone Pisco-sours. Fred liked it so well that he immediately ordered another round. To keep themselves halfway sober they ate some pastries filled with eggs, meat and olives.

Max and Myra went shopping after lunch. Fred and Andrew went out to see the sights and probably get another drink or two. They all agreed to meet back at that restaurant at seven.

Myra was happy that it was just her and Max. She was anxious to go to the curious shops and clothing stores. They were going to check into a hotel at one time but for some reason they forgot about it. Oh well, Myra thought, if we see a hotel on the way back, we can check it out.

Max was happy for the time alone too. His legs were sore from the lack of activity on the boat. He did not want to say anything about his sore legs until after Myra said her legs were sore also. He would never want her to know that he could not do what she could do in the physical department.

They were acting like kids again. They even went down a hill on one of the hill slides. The funiculars reminded them of the cable cars in San Francisco. At around 5:30 Max claimed that he was thirsty and thought it would be a good idea to return to the restaurant and sample some more drinks that were popular in this city. Myra agreed. She saw that Max was suffering. She claimed to be all right. In reality, they were both happy that it was all downhill to the restaurant!

Finally, they made it back to the restaurant. Max ordered something that resembled beer and Myra tried some kind of fruity drink. Max stuck with beer because he always felt in a reasonable amount of control, even after five or six.

The bartender seemed like a knowledgeable fellow, the kind that was half psychologist and half barkeep. The only thing Max could find wrong with him was frequent glances at Myra. Max and the barkeep shared some small talk whenever another beer was brought over. Max asked if he knew the man in the back of the room that was staring in his direction.

The barkeep glanced to the back of the room and then picked up Max's empty. He mumbled something in Spanish and also said 'trouble'. Max told him thanks and tipped him ten dollars. Myra wanted to do a look see to the back of the room but knew it would be a real tell if she did. So, she decided it was time to take a trip to the lady's room. In a stall in the lady's room, she took out her phone and looked at a picture of the boat she had taken the night before. To Myra, it sure looked like the same guy! She was in a big hurry now to get back to Max.

As soon as she sat down, she slid her phone over to Max and told him to look at the picture. Max was shocked, and told Myra she was clever indeed! Max and Myra found themselves in deep thought about why that man was following them. They both were clueless as to whom he might work for.

Max decided to go over and talk to the guy, but Myra held him back with a concerned look and her hand on his arm. She took another glance at the man and decided that he was no match for Max and released her grip on his arm. Max went directly to the man in the back of the room and sat down across from him. In a very clear and deliberate way he asked the man what he wanted. The man replied that he was just having a drink. Max now had his ugly face on, causing the man to give a better reply. He said he was working for a party that was concerned about your activity in this part of the world and would like to know what you were up to.

Max told the man that they were on vacation and also gathering information for a professor in Nebraska on super old people in the Amazon region. He explained that the professor was basically subsidizing his vacation. Max ended the conversation. The guy shrugged his shoulders, blew some smoke in Max's face and walked away.

Max told Myra the conversation and added that if they were in the right place, he would have killed that man before he got a chance to kill any of them. Myra did not doubt Max's sincerity. It took another drink to cool Max down. No one had ever blown smoke in Max's face before.

Max was still trying to calm down when his phone rang. It was Ranger. After their usual crude, brotherly love statements, Ranger got to the point. He wanted to know if Max had a plan firmed up to get the Antifa crap weasels out of the building without destroying the paintings and artifacts.

Max explained that he had it all thought through, but he did not have it down in writing yet. He offered to run through it off the top of his head. Ranger told him to fire away.

Max reiterated the actions they had discussed before-

1. Sealing off the roof.
2. Surrounding the building at a distance with 2000 troops.

3. Allocate two snipers for each window.
4. Numerous fire trucks on hand.
5. Pipe in country music to each floor.
   Max then listed actions that were not previously discussed-
6. There should be twenty soldiers that are experts at 'point and shoot'. Max noted that he would be part of this group. The Ranger said he would be part of this group as well.
7. A 20 mm recoilless rifle to blow the door. It should be located in an armored vehicle.
8. Concussion grenades.
9. Use of experimental bulletproof trench coats.

Max figured that he could have all the Antifa soldiers on the first floor dead within five minutes. Then they would seal the exits to the second floor. They should not fight them in the stairwells; grenades roll down stairwells! They would use this plan on each, floor. He figured that after the second floor, there would be white flags flying from every window above them.

Ranger interrupted at this point saying that 'point and shoot' is the key and they would have to move fast from floor to floor to prevent the enemy from regrouping. He added that 'point and shoot' soldiers were twice as quick to get a shot off than one who aims and also has a better peripheral vision. It was the same technique that the gunslingers of the Old West used. Most of the killing was done within twenty feet.

In conclusion, Ranger said that he didn't need the plan in writing; he would fill in the rough edges. He also said that he knew of an empty building they could practice in. If they could remove Antifa from California, they could make California great again! Ranger emphasized the need for Max to get back, and then made it an order to get back here within two weeks. What he did not tell Max was that other military units were looking to hire Max. Men followed Max! The Department of Justice looked the other way when a General down the line hired Max for a job. Soldiers would follow him into Hell if he asked them to.

Finally, Fred and the crew arrived. Max raised his arms to the bartender to order another round of drinks. There was an extra person with them now though. Max looked long at the new person and Myra stomped on his foot. Max embarrassed himself. He knew there would be a discussion about it later on. He stayed quiet for a while until Myra said she was sorry. He knew though, that she wasn't sorry and there would be no goodnight kiss later when the retired for the night. This was to be Max and Myra's first fight since they got married.

Andrew introduced his girlfriend to Max and Myra. Her name was Camilla. He invited her for dinner. Naturally Max and Myra wanted to know how all this came about, but nothing was being offered. The bartender dropping off drinks and broke the silence. He asked Camilla for her ID and she said that she did not have it with her and gave him an innocent smile.

The barkeep said, "OK!" He then bent down and told her quietly that he was sorry to hear about her mom and dad. Tears immediately flowed from her eyes but she did not give up her smile. Myra saw this but could not quite hear what was said. She motioned to Fred, who was sitting next to Camilla to walk to the other side of the room to talk with her. When Fred arrived, she asked him what the bartender had said. Fred said that he knew her parents and was giving her condolences on their deaths from the plague. Now Myra had to go to the ladies' room to collect her thoughts.

Fred thought he was probably in the clear of trouble for not keeping Andrew from falling in love again. He decided to wait until Myra came out of the ladies' room to finish the story. When Myra returned, he told her that he felt he should tell her about his day. He said that Andrew was trying to work the controls of the funiculars and Camilla showed Andrew how to operate it and somehow her hand found it's way into Andrew's hand and it just stayed there the rest of the day! They had all sat down on a bench and she fell asleep on his shoulder for almost two hours. She was very embarrassed when she woke up. They all had a good laugh. Then her big smile, showing all her perfect teeth, were there again, as if nothing had happened.

Everyone appeared a bit somber when they got back to the table. Myra waved to the bartender to let him know that they wanted to order dinner. Camilla helped them with their Spanish as they ordered. The meals came quickly, they had all ordered something simple. Myra started paying more attention to Camilla. She thought about her parents dying and also noticed Camilla smiling less and once her head bobbed a little like she was falling asleep. She knew what the problem was now. She had the plague. She could not be left alone.

Myra told Max to pay the bill, saying they needed to get Camilla to the boat as soon as possible. This all surprised Max until he looked over at Camilla. She was asleep. Andrew knew there was a problem but did not know what to do. Fred leaned around and told Andrew to pick her up. Fred did not have to tell Andrew twice.

Max handed the bartender two hundred dollars and followed everyone to the door. The bartender saw what happened and didn't want to accept the money but Max insisted. The bartender caught up with them about a block away and handed Max a bottle of Cognac, telling him that he would need it before morning. Max thanked him and thanked him and thanked him!

They were all moving down the street now at a good clip. Max told Fred to stay close to Andrew in case he got exhausted carrying Camilla. After a bit of thinking Fred knew why Max wanted him to carry her next, he finally said to himself, "I can see why he is still married and I've been divorced four times."

Max was pretty proud of himself putting Fred next in line to carry Camilla if need be. 'Myra would show me no mercy toward my goodwill!' There appeared to be no chance of Andrew tiring, he had something in his arms that he was never going to let go of. From time to time, they all heard the preacher's son talking to someone.

Andrew and Fred were the last ones to reach the sailboat. Fred stayed close behind Andrew the whole way. He expected him to drop. Myra was the first to reach the boat. She wanted to change the sheets on the bed in Fred and Andrew's cabin. Fred and Andrew would now be sleeping topside. Myra had given this cabin to Camilla. It was also a way to punish Fred and Andrew.

After laying Camilla on the bed, Andrew collapsed. He could not move his arms for some time. Myra had no pity for a man who thought with his wrong head. She knew this could all turn into a big mess. She chased everyone out of the cabin; no one was going to get a look at Camilla. She made out a list of medicines she needed and gave it to Max.

Max took the list and ran back to where they had dinner. There was still a worker in the place. The worker's English was pretty bad, but he finally got across to Max where the medicine place was located. The worker told Max of a quick way to get there and a long way. Max decided on the quick way, which was not recommended by the worker.

Three men soon jumped Max. They got a few good licks in but after Max sized them up, they all seriously regretted their actions. He kicked each one in the rib cage so they would be out of action for a few weeks. There was no movement when he left, only moaning.

He finally made it to the pharmacy and had some trouble locating the items on the list. A clerk came to assist him. She saw the blood on Max's knuckles and insisted on dressing the wounds. Max told her he hurt his knuckles in a fall. The clerk rolled her eyes.

She looked at the list and had a puzzled look on her face. She asked him why all these items. Max took a chance and told her why. She immediately went to the back room for prescription medicine. She explained how to use the needles, etc. Max let her know that his wife was a nurse, but if she had any questions he would bring her back there. Max thanked her and gave her $200. She thanked him and gave him a hug that lasted too long. He did not want to push her away and make her mad. Max took the long way back to the boat.

Myra was concerned as to why it was taking Max so long. He explained about falling down, which she knew was a lie, most likely a damned lie! But after seeing all that he had brought back, she gave him a long hug. Max started to feel really good about himself.

Myra explained to Max that even with the medicines, she might not be able to save her. If the plague came back completely, she would most certainly die. "Now if we were back in Sausalito, we could take her to that specialist in San Francisco, but we are far away from there and I don't think she has a passport."

Max left the cabin immediately and called Ranger. With unbelievable luck Ranger was there and available to talk to him. He was actually in the process of calling Max. Before Max could get a word out, Ranger said that he needed Max back now! Max said that if he could have one of the C-130's parked over in Santiago swing by, he could be there in two or three days. He mentioned that their pilots could probably use the flying hours anyway. It would be a party of five with one of the passengers being a fifteen-year-old girl without a passport!

There was a bit of a pause and then Ranger replied, "If you get checked for passports it could be a big deal. See what you can do about the passport and get your crew over to Santiago in three days. Ask for a Major Johnson.

Be there several hours or even a day early in case there is a problem. I got to go, take care."

Max could tell Ranger was in a pile of shit and he could not let him down. He went to Myra and told her the plan. He also told her that they needed to find a lawyer immediately. Myra fetched Fred and Andrew and told them the plan. She explained the urgency of getting Camilla to San Francisco. She instructed them to keep an eye on Camilla while she and Max went to find a lawyer.

Chapter 13

Tracy

Myra and Max went to the marina office to see if they could recommend a good lawyer. The manager said that he knew one that was a teacher in the college. He wrote down the lawyer's name and number and let him use the office phone. Max insisted that Myra do the phone call. It took a bit to reach the professor and Myra found him difficult to talk to, but she was a people person with a non-demeaning tone. She explained the problem to him. He told her that it would be very difficult given her time frame. He suggested that Myra contact Tracy at the American consulate in Santiago and gave her the number. Myra politely thanked him just in case she needed to talk to him again.

The call to the consulate took about half an hour. This time the call was being made from Myra's cell phone. The marina manager was showing signs of concern. When she finally got through to this Tracy, she could tell that she was eating something and was probably on an unneeded and unnecessary government break. Myra held her composure and after some cordialities, explained their situation and that the US government was involved etc.

Tracy's response was," Wow! And did you say she was fifteen years old and no living relatives, and very sick with the plague?" Before Myra could reply, Tracy told her to get her young ass married to one of the men in her group.

Myra gritted her teeth and told her that they could have that done by the end of the day. "The husband's name is Andrew Johnson, he is an American citizen and is seventeen years old. His address is 11347 Golden Gate, Sausalito, California.

Tracy told her that they would have to get married immediately! She instructed her to find a Catholic priest and that he would have the paperwork that was required. Myra needed to bring all documentation to Tracy by the next day at four o'clock. Tracy also told her that she had a place lined up for Myra's group to stay the following night. She needed Myra's contact in the Air Force, which Myra promptly gave her. She gave Tracy her cell phone number as well, just in case anything else came up. Tracy told her that she was anxious to see her tomorrow. This was all becoming too much for Myra and she began to feel sick.

Max was quiet. He was still putting it all together and his fist was still hurting. Finally, he came back alive and told Myra to check on Camilla and if everything was ok, they would go back to the place they had eaten in the previous night and see if the bartender knows a priest.

Camilla was sound asleep. Myra gave Andrew and Fred some orders and then she and Max were off. They walked quickly and were soon at the restaurant. Neither of them could remember the bartender's name! Max was happy that he had tipped well last night.

They both ordered a drink and after taking a sip, they found the courage to ask the bartender his name and if he knew a priest. The bartender said his name was Geraldo, and as luck would have it, his brother was a priest. He asked why they were in need of a priest and they spilled the whole unbelievable story.

Geraldo reached for his phone and called his brother. His brother loved weddings and immediately said, "Where and when?"

The question was relayed to Max and Myra, who replied, "At the marina, on a sailboat, today." There was a pause and then Max said," We have no problem with a five-hundred-dollar fee." The priest let them know that he would be there in three hours!

Max asked for another round of drinks. He then invited Geraldo to the wedding. Max and Myra gulped down their drinks and they were off.

Max had trouble keeping up with Myra. She was anxious to see Camilla and explain everything that was going to happen. She wondered too, could

Camilla handle the ceremony? Does she still want to get married to Andrew? If just one thing went wrong, she thought, it is not going to work.

When they reached the boat, Camilla had just woken up. Even with all the medication in her, she looked alert and well. Myra did her best to explain to her all that was going to take place in just a couple hours and again the next day. Camilla appeared to grasp what was going on and that she was going to become a part of this wonderful family/group.

Everyone went to a cabin to clean up and put on their best clothes. Camilla already acted married and told Andrew to run up to her house and bring her a blue dress, her only nice dress, hanging on the closet.

Fred seemed more nervous than everyone. He gave Andrew his wedding ring, the one his ex had thrown at him when she left him. He was giving Andrew advice about everything; after all, he had been married four times!

Everything was starting to move forward. It looked like they would all be presentable and hopefully, present themselves properly. And then Myra's phone rang and it was Tracy. Her first words to Myra were, "You didn't tell me that Andrew's mother didn't know that her oldest son was getting married! I called Peng, his mother, to make sure everything on her son's passport was correct. Well, I got ripped a new one, partly in Mandarin. I know Mandarin and she said some pretty bad things about my mother and me. I answered her in Mandarin and she cleaned up her language very quickly. I think I am going to check and see if Peng is a legal citizen and if she calls me again threatening me, I'm going to scare the hell out of her.

Tracy also talked to Peng's husband, who was very polite, and told Tracy he wanted Fred to call him as soon as possible. Also, we can't find a birth certificate on Camilla. However, I found a Catholic baptismal church record that would make her fifteen!

Myra helped Camilla with her hair and makeup, etc. Max even polished her shoes. Camilla loved the attention everyone was giving her. She also looked very young, even with the makeup Myra put on her.

Myra had Fred selected for the duties of a 'Father of the Bride'. Fred felt very honored. He had been in a wedding party four times before, so he knew exactly what to do.

More people were arriving than expected. Word got out through Geraldo and the manager of the marina. It was soon determined that the boat would be too small and it was also beginning to look like rain. The manager of the marina offered his showroom for the function, which was immediately accepted.

Everyone made it to the marina. There were not enough chairs, but that was all right. The people were in awe of Camilla's beauty. Some of the people knew her age and her circumstances. They wanted the best for her, knowing she would have died there. Everyone was respectful.

Fred did a professional job as 'Father of the Bride'. The priest spoke in Spanish, and that was all right too, everyone knew the marriage process. The rings Fred supplied made the day. The only thing that was a little clumsy was the kiss, because it was their first!

Camilla really hung on to Andrew. People were beginning to notice that Camilla was getting weaker. Myra ushered the married couple back to the boat. Myra helped Camilla put on some night clothes and made her get under the covers. Camilla was soon asleep. Myra gave her an injection, which she hoped would cause her to relax and sleep through the night. Myra gave Andrew a stern order not to get under the covers with her and after everyone left, he would sleep topside.

There was a nice party going on at the marina now. For many, this was the first real party type fun they had since the plague had broken out. Many had brought bottles along and they all knew how to share. The last person left at 10 PM. Max thanked the manager and then told him that he would like to store his boat there for a month or two and that they would be leaving tomorrow. The manager was happy to hear this and gave Max a good deal. Business had been slow since the plague broke out.

When they all got back to the boat, Max told everyone to get ready and put everything away very well because they would be leaving at 9AM the following morning. "We will be transported to Santiago in a van owned by the manager of the marina and on the following day we will be flying to Sausalito."

It was raining now so Fred and Andrew found different places to sleep on the floor and lucky Fred got the sofa. Max buttoned up the boat making it quite cozy inside. Myra redressed Max's knuckle and gave each one a kiss and told him that she loved him.

Myra checked Camilla's vital signs one more time and found her temperature to be one degree above normal. Given all she went through that day probably caused it. She decided to wake her up later and check again. She next checked on Fred to make sure he had a blanket and found him to be ok. She found Andrew sleeping between the stove and the eating counter and noticed that he had a blanket on him but there was no blanket under him. She got another blanket and made him put it on the floor. She also noticed that he was still fully dressed. She told him to take his shirt and jeans off so he could wear them tomorrow and then went to bed.

She found Max snoring. This was something he did when he drank too much. One well-placed elbow put a stop to it.

Myra overslept and was now worried about Camilla's fever. She hurriedly dressed and went to her cabin, which she found empty! She panicked. She went to Fred and shook him until he woke up. "Where is Camilla? She is not in her room!"

Fred knew this would be his fault. He too, had drank too much and headed straight for the sink to get some water. In doing so, he almost stepped on two bodies that were so tangled up it was going to be difficult to get them apart!

So there stood Fred in his shorts and Myra looking at a sight they did not expect to see. There were two piles of clothes, Andrew and Camilla's. This had all happened when Fred was sleeping just ten feet away! Fred put his blanket over them. Myra checked Camilla's forehead and in doing so, noticed that the blankets were full of sweat. Her fever may have broke during their activity.

Myra got one of those thoughts that you believe but if you told anyone they would laugh at you. She believed that Camilla took what was hers and consummated their marriage in the eyes of god. The sweating broke her fever and saved her life. In a sort of way, it was what happened to Max and Myra back in Omaha.

Myra went back to her cabin and hung on tightly to Max. She could not go back to sleep.

In the morning, it was rush, rush and rush. Myra handed Camilla a towel and pointed towards the shower. Not a word was said to each other, but Myra was reading a slight smile on Camilla's face. Myra wanted to spank her, that's what you do to fifteen-year-olds!

Andrew kept away form Myra the best he could. Fred gave him some aftershave lotion to put on. They both stood outside with a bag of clothes and waited for the bus. It was a very beautiful drive to Santiago. Due to road conditions, it took almost three hours to get there.

Camilla and Andrew sat in the very rear seat. Whenever Myra turned around she noticed they still could not keep their hands off each other. About an hour into the trip, Camilla was fast asleep. After another hour, Andrew was too.

They arrived at the consulate one hour early. Myra had given everyone a lecture on how to conduct them selves. Camilla appeared nervous but kept a smile on her gorgeous face. Fred tried to keep out of the view of Myra.

Tracy called everyone into her office. She started off by saying that she really did not need to see everyone but was curious as to what this group actually looked like. There was a pause and then she looked at Andrew and told him that he need to talk to his mother but recommended that he wait and do it in person because she did not think that if he told her over the phone that it would be believed. "I think it's going to take a long time for you to smooth things over with your mother.

She then addressed Fred and told him that he should avoid Andrew's mother altogether. "She said she was going to do bad things to you."

Now she looked back at Max and said," You don't remember me but I remember you. I was in Afghanistan covering for a sick diplomat. I happened to be in the right place at the wrong time and had to help make a report on a battle scene that at first glance, almost made me throw up. Your arms were covered in blood up to your elbows. This soldier they referred to as Ranger told me quite a few lies to keep you out of Leavenworth prison. He even threatened to put me on active duty to help stop and advancing enemy force. He said that without Max, the position couldn't be held. I signed the report exonerating you from executing wounded enemy soldiers. I was a coward at the time but no longer regret doing so. Part of why I'm approving this passport for Camilla is because I would have to deal with you if I didn't"

She now addressed Camilla. "You say you are 18. You are not 18! Camilla opened her mouth to say something but quickly closed it. Tracy said, "I have made some phone contacts in the area where Camilla lived and they all make you out to be a good person. The priest even claims someone with a higher authority had to have watched over you and guided you through all of this. Proof of this is that you didn't argue when I said you weren't 18. If you had, I would not have signed for your passport! Also, your smile is going to open a lot of doors for you. If you use it to open the wrong doors, I will revoke your passport.

She now addressed Myra again and told her to lead this group to the C-130 warming up outside and to do it before she changed her mind!

Much hugging took place and then the exhausted group followed Max and Myra to the plane. When they were all aboard the plane, Myra looked at Camilla's passport and saw that it listed her age at 18.

Captain Johnson introduced himself to everyone. He apologized for the seating configuration. All of the passenger seats were attached by hooks to the sidewalls of the airplane, leaving the center open for cargo. During the plague, the U.S. flew in tons of food, medicine and body bags. Unfortunately for Camilla and Andrew, it left them totally exposed for the next ten hours.

The four large propeller engines on the C-130 sharply accelerated and soon they were in the air. Max, seeing the seating configuration, reminded him of the time he and his team were dropped behind enemy lines in Afghanistan. He imagined it would not be long he would be dropped behind enemy lines again, but this time on a contract assignment. He also thought about Ranger and the contract assignment at the tar pits. He felt it would be a shame if the priceless pictures and artifacts were destroyed by those crap weasels. However, Max wondered if it was worth a couple hundred of our soldiers dying to save those pictures. 'If my plan works', he thought, 'there will be few of our soldiers killed'.

Max went over his plan in his mind again. He knew the timing on everything had to be perfect. He also knew the Ranger would not let him down in the training area. He also planned to not take any prisoners and hoped Ranger would not get in his way. He felt those crap weasels should not live to fight another day and also that they shouldn't be poisoning the minds of other men in jail.

Myra noticed the distorted expressions on Max's face and she shook him. She received a smile for her action. Max said he saw a man kiss her in a dream. Myra always knew when Max was not telling the truth. It made her upset when he kept things from her.

Max went up and sat in the co-pilot's seat for a while. The pilot and Max shared war stories with each other. Some would say the two of them were telling lies, but if they knew Max, they would think it was all an understatement.

Max informed Johnson that he was a contract worker for the military. Johnson said that he had flown for some contract work before. He said he always did it with his modified/restored C-130. He felt it was the best damn cargo plane ever made. He spent many dollars and hours restoring the old C-130. He had only one project left and that was to change out the brakes. The brake pads were getting thin, but so far still worked well.

Max told Johnson he was sending his wife, Myra, up to keep you company for a while, and to please do not talk to her about contract work. He also said to send her back in about a half hour.

Myra was surprised that he would let her sit up front with Johnson. Max had become more and more possessive of her lately. At the wedding, she saw him becoming angry when one of the male guests had a long and sort of private conversation her. Maybe it was the wine Max had been drinking, but he scolded her later, which did not end well. Max later knew that he had been wrong and now he was trying to change things. Max was anxious for her return.

After Myra returned, Max had Camilla and Andrew wet up front. Andrew sat in the co-pilot's chair and Camilla stood in between the two of them. It could have been the medication or the long sleep she had, but Camilla was energized. She had never seen so many instruments and gauges before. The questions would not stop and Andrew soon felt that he was no longer part of the group. Johnson was very happy to have the co-pilot return from his rest period. He told Andrew and Camilla to return to their seats.

Andrew was upset and felt less important to Camilla than the pilot. Camilla was winding down from her medication and no longer full of energy. Somewhere in this process she realized she had acted like a kid and not a married woman. Fear came over her that Andrew would not want her anymore. When they got back to their seats, she put both hands on Andrew's arm, squeezing tightly until she fell asleep.

All of this did not go without notice by Myra. She checked the time and noticed that Camilla was an hour overdue for her injection. Camilla slept right through the injection. Myra informed Andrew that she was very high on drugs right now and might not know what she is doing. She grabbed a blanket from a nearby chair and gave Andrew orders to keep her warm and let her sleep.

Myra was concerned about Camilla's ups and downs. She could not stabilize the blood pressure and temperature. There were three hours yet to go. She had the doctor's phone number who she was taking Camilla to see. She went to Captain Johnson and asked him which airport they would be landing at and when would she be able to use her phone.

Johnson informed Myra that they would be landing at Oakland in less than three hours and that she should be able to use her cell phone now. If it didn't work, he told her she could use his phone. She informed the Captain that there was an emergency with Camilla and that she had to monitor her vitals every fifteen minutes.

Fred was wanting to do something to help. He sat down on the other side of Camilla, thinking that if she wanted her daddy, all she had to do was grab his arm. One old man was the same as another, he thought.

Myra was successful in contacting the specialist, Doctor Meier. He was well briefed by Myra, who was starting to get emotional. The doctor told her that if Camilla's pulse started slowing down, she must wake her up and make her walk around. He went on to say that a relapse is very critical. The patient, at this point, often wants to die. He let her know that there would be an ambulance waiting at the runway.

Chapter 14

The Inca Princess

The doctor was concerned that Myra was becoming emotional. As he was giving Myra orders, he told her that there would be no more dying of the plague in his hospital. "Don't let up! Do what you were trained to do!"

Max went up to the cockpit and informed the Captain of the situation. Before Max finished the sentence, Johnson pushed the throttle all the way forward into the redline area. The engines were screaming as they headed through a large thunderhead cloud, which procedure would have had them fly around. He put the seatbelt lights on.

Somehow, the press picked up this emergency flight. Everyone was buying the newspapers and listening to there TVs and radios in Chile and the U.S. They wanted to find out about the Inca Princess on an emergency flight to America!

They were now only a half hour from Oakland. The airport was closed to all flights except the C-130 they were on.

The church council at Ron's church set up a prayer vigil and ordered Peng, Ron, and Matt to go to the hospital.

The wheels touched down for a perfect landing, except they came in way too fast. He burned out all four brakes getting the C-130 stopped only feet from the end of airport runway! The ambulance and fire trucks headed for the plane, which had smoking brakes! Myra, Camilla and Andrew were snatched up and taken to the Oakland Bay Bridge, sirens blaring all the way.

There was a line-up of doctors and nurses at the emergency entrance of the hospital. All doctors were on duty, just in case they were needed for any type of emergency.

Now all they could do was wait. All family and close friends were ushered to a waiting room. A couple of reporters disguised as friends made it to the room but were quickly shown the door. In the end, Peng was too confused to be angry with anyone.

About two hours later, Doctor Meier came in and addressed them. There was no smile on his face. He said that they needed a lot of blood from Max. Not only did he have the same blood type as Camilla, but he had other genetic factors in his blood that only 130 other people in the world had. We also need blood from type O people. We should have blood available but because of the heavy fighting going on in Los Angeles, we had to send our blood there. We will need three people. We start pumping blood into Max's leg after we have removed half a gallon from his arm and put that into Camilla's arm. A total of one gallon of blood is needed from Max. Max weighs about 220 pounds so he should be able to do this.

The doctor concluded by saying that it was a very dangerous procedure that had not been tried before. I cannot make anyone do this, he said, but we need four people with type O blood." Four people immediately stood up.

The doctor started to open the door and instead turned around and asked Camilla if she had any living relatives. There was no response.

Max and Myra departed form the operating room. She informed the doctor that she was a registered nurse and that she would be by her husband. The four volunteers followed a few minutes later, after talking to Pastor Ron. The blood was checked for accuracy. Myra noticed that Peng was first in line. She also noticed that Camilla was on life support.

The delicate procedure of pumping and injecting blood into a patient at the same time is seldom practiced because of the risks that may be encountered. According to Doctor Meier though, it should work. Max was holding out all right but was starting to get pains in his chest. There was a fear now that he could panic. The two doctors working on Max were well qualified. They knew exactly what to watch for. Doctor Meier concentrated entirely on Camilla because she was on life support.

Towards the end, several nurses were called in to aid the two doctors working on Max. They assisted in strapping him down. The doctors and nurses were becoming fearful of him. Also, the things he was saying to them were extremely horrible. They wondered what kind of man could risk death and kill at will on the field of battle and now help a girl he had only known for a few days.

Camilla's vital signs were all in the safety zones. Doctor Meier knew he was not home yet though. His appearance showed a high level of concentration and sweat beading up on his brow. He finally reached the point where he knew he could do no more. Everyone exited the room except for one nurse to monitor Camilla.

Max either passed out or fell asleep after the ordeal. After about an hour he woke up. He noticed the nurse was completing paperwork and turning his aching head to the other side, he observed Camilla staring in his direction. She didn't have the energy to say anything but her infectious smile was back!

After another hour or so, Max was getting restless but he wasn't able to stand up. He asked the nurse for a phone. The nurse knew he would not be able to handle the phone but she gave it to him anyway. After embarrassing himself, he asked her to make the call to Ranger for him. She smiled and made the call.

Ranger answered and soon realized that the slurry voice was Max. He told Max that he had been following his ordeal as it periodically came out on the news. He then told Max that he had some very good news, which was the surrender of the Antifa forces holed up in the tar pit complex. I used your plan of circling the area with a large number of soldiers and aiming a 20mm cannon at the front door. It must have scared them because they were soon waving the white flag! Your plan worked! Your check is in the mail. Go back to sleep. Max was very happy that the tar pit battle was resolved peacefully. He was also happy that he was going to receive full payment, as per the contract!

Fred saw Myra and Peng talking together in the back of the waiting room. They both gave Fred the 'why are you bothering me' look. Fred said that he would like for Andrew and Camilla to live with him at his house. Myra and Peng now gave Fred the 'dead pan' look! Fred ignored their crude gestures and said that those two should be alone and making decisions together. I am an old man who will keep a stable atmosphere in place and you two will smother them. They won't even be able to have a good fight! Myra and Peng felt insulted and hunted for words they could use to dismiss him. Fred got the picture and returned to his corner.

Myra was the first to say that her and Max would likely be travelling a lot and was not sure if she wanted Max to be her father figure. Then Peng retorted that she did not have enough room and she noticed Matt's tongue had been hanging out of his mouth ever since he saw Camilla. She hoped that he understood that brothers couldn't share all the toys! They both motioned to Fred at the same time.

Fred slowly came back, expecting to be ostracized again. He was amazed to find that they had accepted his offer. They also told him that they would go over to his house and clean up for him.

When Andrew found out, he was ecstatic. This was a very big load off his shoulders.

Andrew was the first person allowed to come in to the room to see his wife. She saw him coming and they were in a tongue lock in no time. Max turned his head so he did not view it. It caused him a lot of pain to turn his head. All he wanted right now was a cold PBR.

Andrew informed Camilla that they had injected a gallon of Max's blood into her, which the doctors said made Max her brother. Camilla's eyes opened very wide. She did not know if it was true or not. Andrew said that his mother was very anxious to come in and comb her hair and wipe her face. There was a panic attack about to happen and then Camilla said," Okay."

Peng soon arrived and was so excited that she started talking in Mandarin. Andrew had to calm her down some and then the two of them tried to communicate, Camilla with a Spanish accent and Peng with a Mandarin accent.

When Peng got back to the waiting room, she elaborated on their conversation, to include that Camilla was very young and she would have to be more than just a mother-in-law now.

Fred came in next and talked with Max first. Max wanted Fred to sneak him a PBR. Fred smiled and told him that it would be difficult but he would try. Fred then went over to Camilla and touched the side of her face. She could not see Fred but she knew who it was. This made Fred feel very good indeed. He then left the room to go on his beer run.

Ron came in last and walked over to Max. He thanked Max for taking care of Andrew and increasing the size of his family. He also said that Myra needed to reopen the clinic and maybe Camilla could work there too. Max acknowledged his request/advice.

Ron then met Camilla. He welcomed her to the family. Camilla knew that getting Ron's approval was important and she reached for his hand. While holding her hand, he said a prayer for her, knowing she was a Catholic; he also made a sign of the cross.

Due to Myra being a registered nurse, both Camilla and Max were released at the end of the following day. The nurse that helped Max with his phone call saw an opportunity to tell him that she regretted being rude to him and told him that she would help him make a phone call anytime he needed help. She also stated that she didn't know who he was when she first met him. She found out that he was a celebrity and the man that saved California from the Antifa gangs. She then advised him to not try to save California all by himself! "Remember the retired people of Berkeley and Quyen won the Battle of Berkeley Hills. Great things are done by many small things put together."

The nurse seemed overwhelmed by standing next to Max and suddenly grabbed him and gave him a kiss. Camilla saw it all, especially when his weak arm slid down her back!

Max was actually too weak to have prevented the kiss. On the way back to Sausalito, Max wondered if he should tell Myra what happened. There was only one witness, and why would Camilla cause problems? Max decided not to tell Myra; after all, he did not return the kiss.

Camilla was in wonderment at all she saw in San Francisco. Fred gave them a quick tour of the city, to include the "most Crooked Street in the World", China Town, Fisherman's Wharf, the cable cars, and then on the way out, the Golden Gate Bridge.

Everyone was pointing out sights for Camilla to see. Finally, they entered the city of Sausalito. Fred stopped at the marina and made sure that Max and Myra made it into the building okay. He then drove home with Andrew and Camilla.

They all took it easy for the next couple of days. Myra was considering the possibility of opening up the clinic again. Possibly she could train Camilla to be her assistant and when business was slow, she could work on a correspondence course to earn a GED. She decided to talk to Peng about this. It is always best to keep the whole family involved.

Matt had kept himself busy doing research on the conspiracy theories that were interesting Max and Andrew. He used his computer and listened to a radio station that discussed variations of these theories. Matt was anxious to review his work with Max.

Max was never a hundred percent believer in these theories, however, since someone with a Luger tried to kill him and Myra, he became more interested.

Matt had his findings very well organized. To keep him and Max on the same page, he listed the most talked about theories as follows-

1. There is a 'red pill', which enables you to sharply increase the length of your life.
2. German military and government officials smuggled gold bars to an unknown location in South America.
3. The plague was now deemed man made and the first known case that was officially found was in the northern reaches of the Amazon.

Matt went and tackled number one first. He said the radio station that follows the sightings of people who should be dead has a listing of 157 people that had been seen by more than two people. Not included on this list was the man with the Luger that had tried to kill Max and Myra. The fingerprints on the gun were from a man born in 1918. That verification had come from Interpol. Matt noted that Ranger had helped him with this.

The second theory that certain Germans smuggled gold bars out of Germany had not been proven. Their whereabouts had not been established. However, the upper reaches of the Amazon seemed to be the best guess. Also, an Indian tribe reported that there was a building high in the Andes that could possibly be their headquarters. Most of the building had been demolished in an earthquake. A mining company killed off the tribe that gave the story.

The country of Brazil had officially proved the third theory.

In conclusion, Matt felt the first theory had been proven as far as he was concerned. There was nothing more they could do with it anyway. He recommended checking out the second theory. The third had been proven.

Max sat quietly for a couple of minutes and then asked Matt to hear him out on the conspiracy theories and the idea of finding gold bars and maybe the source of the red pill in the Amazon. He then praised his work for it's excellent organization but noted that they still didn't have the smoking gun that would absolutely prove any of this out. He went on about how the upper reaches of the Amazon contained several thousands of square miles and without a positive clue it would be impossible to find what they were after. It would be like finding a needle in a haystack.

Max felt that Matt would be more productive if he found positive proof that Soros was financing this and in control of Antifa. "To do this", he said, "it would probably be a good idea to work for a degree at Berkeley or Pepperdine University. While you are earning your degree, which you need anyway, you could befriend students associated with Antifa. Note that your surname is not the same as mine. There is danger in this plan so you need to keep your eyes wide open! Also, it would be a good idea to talk to Ranger. He may want to put you through a short class on how to do this kind of work. I suspect he will pay you for your work."

Once Max used the word 'Ranger', Matt was all ears. The two worked together on the corpse from Muir Woods. Matt left the meeting feeling pretty good. Max called the Ranger to give him a heads up.

Max walked over to Fred's house to see how things were going. Fred was up and had already made coffee. Camilla then stumbled out of the bedroom when she heard Max and Fred talking and got a cup of coffee. She was in very skimpy clothes. When she walked by Max he slapped her on the rear and informed her that when he was in the house she will have proper clothes on! "You are not a little girl anymore!"

Max got up and told Fred he would come back another day. He was not very upset. Part of what he had done was for Fred's benefit. He needed to let those two young adults he was supervising know what kind of standards would have to be adhered to in his house. He also mentioned to Fred, "What would happen if Myra or Peng had come over this morning?" This got Fred's attention.

When Max got back to the marina, Myra was eating her breakfast. Her shorts looked a little tight also so he slapped her on the rear too! Only Myra did not get upset. It was obvious that she liked it. She did say though, "You should not do that to other women!"

Max got a sudden sick feeling in his stomach. The nurse and Camilla flashed through his mind. Maybe he was a very bad person. Maybe it was good that he wasn't raising a child of his own.

Chapter 15

Camilla and Myra Are Pregnant

Myra informed Max that she had a doctor's appointment that morning. She said that she had been very tired of late. Max suggested that she take Camilla along and give Fred a break. That sounded good to Myra. They could ride the cable cars together.

Max said that he would stay at the marina and get some paperwork finished and also contact Ranger.

Myra took the long drive into San Francisco to see the doctor. It was a beautiful day. There was a wait at the doctor's office, which gave them some time for girl talk.

Camilla told her that Max got upset with her at Fred's place that morning. She told Myra about how she wasn't properly dressed when she came out to get a cup of coffee and that she was wearing one of Andrew's shirts without any underwear, but the shirt covered everything. "He whacked me and sent me back to my room! Fred talked to me about it again after Max left. The day did not start out very well for me."

Myra wanted to know if he hurt her head when he hit her. Camilla said "no". Luckily for everyone concerned, the nurse came in and called Myra's name.

Myra informed the doctor that she was a registered nurse and should be able to diagnose her own health problems, but being this tired all the time is a different kind of problem than I normally have when my period is late. She also informed him that she could not have children and showed him the scar where the doctor had operated.

The doctor did the usual procedures to include getting a urine sample, which was immediately used for a pregnancy test. The doctor's prognosis was correct! Myra nearly went into shock. A nurse took her next door for a sonogram. The result was as expected for pregnancy. It also confirmed that, for whatever reason, Doctor Thorpe did not go through with the operation.

When Myra got back to the waiting room, Camilla was not there. The receptionist said that she was in the bathroom. Myra waited a bit and then decided to check and see if Camilla was okay. She was in the process of vomiting. Myra was very concerned that maybe this had something to do with the plague and explained this to the receptionist who immediately went and got the doctor.

The doctor did a quick examination and said that he was going to call Doctor Meier that had handled the plague relapse ordeal. Doctor Meier wanted Camilla back at his hospital immediately.

Everyone at the doctor's office knew that Camilla was the Inca Princess from Chile. They all recognized her from the news reports. When the ambulance arrived, the doctor and Myra went along with her to the hospital. At the hospital, Camilla's was stabilized pretty quickly. Doctor Meier said it was too soon to tell, but she may be pregnant! He also suggested not telling her, because she probably wasn't. He wanted her to stay overnight just to be safe.

Myra checked the news to kill some time at the hospital. The breaking news came on. The headline read as follows:

THE INCA PRINCESS IS BACK IN THE HOSPITAL. SHE WAS FOUND VOMITING IN A BATHROOM. RECORDS SHOW THAT SHE IS EITHER 13, 15 OR 18 YEARS OLD. THERE COULD BE LEGAL ACTION AGAINST THE FATHER, WHO IS 18. THERE COULD ALSO BE LEGAL ACTION AGAINST THE AMERICAN CONSULATE IN SANTIAGO, CHILE.

Further on in the article it said that a Tracy Moran, the head of the American consulate in Chile, was on her way to San Francisco to clean up this mess. She claimed to have an official Catholic baptismal document to back up the age of 18.

Back in San Francisco, there were hundreds of reporters now standing in the rain outside of the hospital.

Myra was so anxious to let everyone in Sausalito know that she was pregnant, and now this tart was sucking all of the oxygen out of the room. And looking across the room, Camilla sat with that big infectious smile.

Camilla was extremely popular throughout California. Her story was followed by almost everyone. The mayor, up for re-election in San Francisco, vowed to protect her from any group that would try to send her back to Chile.

Tracy arrived early the next morning to meet with the mayor of San Francisco and the district judge. At stake was the validity of Camilla's Catholic baptismal document. An atheist organization was contesting the document, saying that the ink on the paper appeared wet! It was outrageous to hear these obviously dishonest attacks being made on Camilla!

After Tracy met with the mayor and district judge, a publicity statement was worked up to support Camilla and her husband Andrew. A picture of Camilla, Andrew, the mayor, the district judge and Tracy was circulated in the press shortly thereafter. Poll numbers for the mayor jumped 20 points!

The atheist group discontinued their efforts after determining the legal action costs. Money being supplied by a Soros fund to aid the atheist group soon evaporated. To sew this matter up, the district judge proclaimed that the baptismal record did not have to be released by the church.

Tracy's popularity mushroomed! Political power brokers in San Diego pressured her to run for mayor. She was actively considering it.

An undercover audit by Tracy's DC boss on forged documents found in a file safe in her office had nothing to do with her considering running for mayor. The audit was soon dropped for publicity reasons. It appeared that Tracy was being offered early retirement!

All the commotion in San Francisco finally calmed down. Myra picked up Camilla from the hospital after Doctor Meier released her. Also, Doctor Meier confirmed that Camilla was indeed pregnant. He gave them the name of a baby doctor they could both use in the Sausalito area. He said that he had worked with this doctor at one time and felt that his skill as a baby doctor was among the best.

On the way back home, Myra felt that the doctor was more concerned with Camilla's baby than with hers. She felt as though she was always playing second fiddle to her!

Finally, Myra broke the silence and asked Camilla in a very friendly, joking way, about Max whacking her on the butt because of her attire in Fred's house.

Camilla was, once again, very coy with her reply, "saying that he had got her attention and she put more clothes on."

Myra could not pursue this matter further without it being obvious what it was that she wanted to find out. They sat there in silence the rest of the way home. They both went inside when they got to Fred's house. Myra remarked to Fred how clean and organized he was keeping the house.

Myra found a chance to talk one on one with Fred. His reply to her request was that he was pouring coffee at the time when Max hit her, seemed rehearsed!

Myra left and drove up the street to the marina. During this short drive, she planned how she was going to present this whacking Camilla on the butt story again without appearing obsessed or silly or jealous about the whole matter. As they say, 'let sleeping dogs lie.' Well, she did not! She decided to trick Max.

Myra walked over to Max and said that Camilla told her that he had slapped her on her partially exposed posterior. Max tried to reply but did a poor job of choosing his words and said something to the effect of he did not intend to hit her there and that he had a cup of coffee in his other hand etc. They both looked directly at each other and Max concluded by, "he was trying to burn the whole thing from his mind".

Maybe it was because she was pregnant and her emotions were not under control, but she started swinging away. They both ended on the bed and after some bad name calling by Myra, they indulged in 'make up sex'.

Max and Myra walked to the boardwalk near the marina in the late afternoon. It was almost the end of summer and it was perfectly beautiful outside. They sat down on the same bench they were on when the assassin had tried to kill them. Max noted that Alcatraz looked the same now as it did back then. He suggested that when they got their boat back from Valparaiso, they should sail around the prison landmark. They both agreed that since they had met, their lives were blessed.

Max said that they should fly to Valparaiso the next day and get their boat. He also explained what Matt was going to do and to not tell that to anyone else. They also discussed Andrew's future. They felt that it would be wonderful if Camilla became a nurse and Andrew became a doctor. It was agreed that Myra would discuss this idea with Peng.

Max made reservations for the two of them to fly out of Oakland the next morning at 6 am.

Before Max and Myra flew to Valparaiso, he called Ranger to let him know where he would be if needed. Ranger knew they were going to sail their boat back home when they were free to do so. Max told Ranger they are going to trade their sailboat in for a motorboat if they could find a good deal. He added that because of the economic conditions and the high price of fuel, the locals were trading in their motorboats for sailboats.

Ranger said he thought it would be a good idea to get a fast motorboat. The sailboats were slow and required a lot of work. He added, "If you do trade, remove the monitor from the sailboat and attach it to the new boat in an inconspicuous place."

It was a long flight to Valparaiso. There were no direct or non-stop flights, which was the main problem. Max's contract work with Ranger was paying very well, so they flew first class, which gave them a degree of privacy and better comfort. It actually ended up being two days to get all the way back to Santiago. They stopped in to see Johnson while they were in Santiago. He had a hangar at the airport with a number of planes he was restoring. One of the planes was a Cessna 172 Pontoon. It was his baby and he had a vacation with it planned.

Finally, Max and Myra reached the marina. The owner of the marina was happy to see them and for them to see the '58 Sea Ray Sundancer. He told them he could switch boats for only $120,000. Myra and Max felt it was a reasonable price. Max asked if the boat was debt free and the marina owner said that it was and provided the paperwork from a reputable title company.

It was a big decision for them, but finally they took a deep breath and said they would take it. This was the first big purchase they had made in their marriage.

Within an hour the paperwork was completed. Max was then given one-on-one instructions on the mechanics of the boat. Max was still a little apprehensive about the idea of going on such a long trip in a boat he knew very little about.

Myra said that she was not worried; after all, the sailboat had gone many miles on just a motor too.

Max purchased five containers of fuel as a safety. He also took the tracking device off of the sailboat and attached it to his new boat. He called it a new boat but it was actually two years old. He saw a few scratches and marks that he could fix when they got back to Sausalito. Myra soon returned from the tienda next door. She had bought nearly $300 of food for the trip.

The marina owner suggested that they had better be on their way because of a storm that was coming from the south. They heeded his advice and with tears in their eyes, said good-bye to their sailboat and they were off.

The new boat was much faster than their sailboat. The waters were calm as they headed out into the evening. The lighting system was great, giving them remarkable visibility. Soon the moon was up and they were becoming more comfortable with their boat.

They saw the storm behind them and were not troubled by it, due to the speed of their boat. They decided to stay about fifty miles from the coast at all times. Myra saw something in the water ahead of them that appeared strange. Max was looking at it now too and noticed something like a can and was always pointing towards them as they came closer. Myra slowed the boat down to get a better look and noticed it was fixed on something dark below. Max had already determined what it was and looked back to the bench next to him and sees if his .45 was there. He found it and stuck it in his belt.

Max told Myra to cut the motor and to turn the light on the submarine. As she turned the light on the submarine it slowly raised out of the water and a lid near the lookout pipe started to open. A man started to come out carrying a large automatic weapon. Max told him to get rid of the gun or get shot. The man turned quick to shoot, but Max dropped him and he slid into the water. Two more men tried to stick their heads out saying, "Don't Shoot!" As soon as they could though, they tried to take aim and Max shot them both. At this range, Max could not miss. Those two men also slid into the water. He heard one of them saying something in Spanish.

The side of their boat and the side of the submarine were now touching. Max stepped onto the sub and closed the lid to prevent a possible wave of water rushing in. He then thought that maybe someone else was in there so he partially raised the lid and yelled inside. There was no response. He did not have the courage nor the stupidity to climb down inside. He would be defenseless.

He told Myra to contact Ranger with the boat phone. Myra made contact and handed the phone to Max. Max in turn, handed the .45 to Myra and told her to keep her eye of the sub's lid.

Max went over everything that had happened to them including their location. Ranger wanted to know how long the sub was and Max guessed it to be around sixty feet. Ranger said it was too small to be a military sub, so that pretty much made it a drug smuggling sub. He went on to say that it must be out of order. Do you have an anchor rope or chain?

Max said that they did and also that he had noticed a hook on the nose of the sub that they could tie onto. What do you want me to do?

Well, Ranger said, you can pull the sub but it will go slow and take a long time and use a lot of fuel. Let me check with the Navy for advice and I'll call you back.

Ranger called back shortly saying that the Navy had no assets anywhere near Max's location. He also told Max that the Navy didn't have the manpower to get involved in drug trafficking. Max told Ranger he would phone Johnson and see if he could bring fuel and a .50 caliber sniper rifle. Ranger expressed to Max that he shouldn't phone Johnson because his phone had been compromised.

Max got a wild idea then. "Remember Tracy?" he asked, "Well, she is a linguist. He could contact her in a language that the cartels are not likely to know. Also, Tracy has a secure line for diplomats to use. She could contact Johnson, who has a Cessna in Santiago. It would take him about two hours to get here. He could carry 50 gallons of fuel. After delivery, he would have to return to a spot a couple hundred miles up the coast and repeat. Each time he would return to the coast a little farther up, fill up the fuel cans and then return."

Ranger agreed with Max's plan. Max was to call Tracy and speak in the Farsi' language' and then Tracy was to call the Ranger and Johnson on the secure line. Ranger also gave Tracy additional information as to the exact location of Max and to bring him a .50 caliber sniper rifle. The Ranger added, "If the sub's ears were working, you will be in for a lot of trouble." Also, the sub is either full of drugs or cash, depending on witch direction it was going. Don't even think about what has to have crossed your mind concerning the money. The cartel will hunt you down or our own government could have a place for you at Leavenworth!

Max placed a call to Tracy, who was in the process of driving on the interstate in San Diego at a very high speed, which she knew she could get away with, because of her diplomatic immunity. After some affectionate, unprintable remarks, they got down to business. He informed her that he was going to give her a message in a foreign language. She was then to give the message to Ranger in English on her protected line. Ranger would then tell her what to communicate to Johnson on the protected line.

Tracy pulled over into a rest area and wrote down the message that Max gave her in Farsi. She informed Max that he had just ruined her scheduled lunch with someone she had just met! She also mentioned that Max's use of that language was very poor. Also, it sounds to me like you've gotten yourself into another mess. Take care.

Max soon noticed that he was not making very good progress moving the sub and it would only get worse as he reached the equator, because of the current running north to south. Also, an idiot light indicated that the engines were running hot. He knew this was not going to work. He decided to practice his Farsi with Tracy again!

Conversation with Tracy, translated from Farsi: "My boat is too small to move the sub and the engine is running hot. When Johnson arrives, I plan to scuttle the sub after I've determined that there is no one left on board. Also, if the sub has a large quantity of money on board, I suggest we remove the money and turn it in to the proper authorities. This process of turning in the money should be handled by you and appear in the media. In this way, I'm thinking the cartel will not come after us for the money. In conclusion, I do not think five people, which include two women, would be able to keep this a secret, if we tried to handle the money, if that's the case, in a different way. Please advise.

Tracy was upset with the message. She could use the money, if the sub had bundles of it, to fund her campaign. She told Max that she was not afraid of the cartel and she was always 'packing'.

Max informed Tracy that if the cartel got ahold of her, which they would, she would beg them to kill her.

After this conversation, Tracy checked her purse for her .45 caliber hand cannon and moved it to a place under her dress. She also hired a bodyguard, which a lot of politicians do anyway. She did not like what Max had said about the cartel. She did not like Max, period. She planned to talk to Ranger about that chicken Max!

It was a joy for both of them to see Johnson coming in for a landing on the water. The ocean was like glass, which made it look very easy. Myra had a meal prepared and with the sun on their backs, they had a pleasant time partaking breakfast.

They discussed the situation at hand. The decision was pretty much made by Max, but he wanted everyone's approval.

The first task was to put as much fuel into the boat's tanks as was possible and set the remaining can on top of the sub. The water was so calm; the spillage of fuel was not even in question.

The next task was interrupted by a return message from Tracy. She informed them that Max's plan was agreeable with him. He wished Max good luck with the inspection at hand.

All three climbed on top of the sub and positioned themselves around the entrance. A rope was tied around Max just in case if the worst happened. Max now climbed down the ladder into the sub, using one hand. The other hand was firmly holding his .45. There was great concern on Max's face. Myra was shaking so much that she was almost useless. Max was greatly relieved when he reached the floor. The first compartment was filthy and smelled very bad. The engine room/control area was a little cleaner, but it still smelled bad. Max was concerned with the putrid air, but he continued on.

He now ventured toward the compartment in the rear of the sub. Here he found two young women tied up and with tape covering their mouths. Their wrists were bleeding. He could tell that they were still alive but their heads hung down and their eyes were closed.

Max took the rope and tied it around the first girl and moved her to the exit ladder. He stopped then, and using his cell phone camera, took multiple pictures of the entire scene. He then jerked on the rope along with yelling instructions to hoist the girl up.

Max pushed on the girl from below and soon had her topside. He did not instruct Myra on what to do, as she was a nurse. He did protrude his head through the opening once in a while for some fresh air. He saw Myra remove the clothes from the girl, which was just a large shirt, and with Johnson's help, lowered her into the ocean for a bath. Eventually they untied the rope from her and got her back on the boat. As Max pulled the rope back to him, he could see the young woman coughing. He could also see that Johnson and Myra worked very well together. He wondered why that thought entered his head. His life was far from perfect before he met Myra and this could be his karma.

Max repeated the procedure with the second young woman, only she was not as warm as the first and she had a white substance coming out of her mouth. He actually said a prayer quietly over her. As he turned to move her out, he found Myra standing next to them. He had not heard her arrive.

Myra ran to the ladder and yelled to Johnson to get her medical kit sitting on the boat where they had cleaned up the first woman. Myra received the kit in no time flat. She immediately injected some adrenalin into her. Then hoisted her to the top and then over to the boat, skipping the clean up step. Myra somehow kept her alive. It was very intense. She kept blowing into the woman's lungs, making her vomit, everything she had seen the boss she hated, Doctor Thorpe, do to save the lives of junkies.

Alarmingly, she found the other young woman standing next to her. She pulled on Myra's shirt and said in broken English, "Her mother's name is Mateo." They both found themselves saying "Mateo, Mateo, Mateo." To Myra's surprise, the dying young woman's eyes opened for a few seconds. The girl changed her mind about dying and made a desperate run for her life. Both Myra and the other woman kept talking to her as they were cleaning her up. If her eyes closed they made a terrible fuss over her. This was all too much for Johnson so he went down to help Max.

Max and Johnson made a thorough search of the sub. Everything was checked except a small room in the bow of the sub, which was locked. They both discussed what could happen if they beat the door down with some heavy tools lying about. The room could very well be booby-trapped!

Max ordered Johnson to go topside. Johnson replied that Max was not in the military and he could stick his order up his ass. At this point, Johnson gave Max a sucker punch. It rocked Max but it didn't knock him down. Johnson had done some fighting in his day and knew that he was in for a terrible beating if he did not leave. Johnson fled topside.

Johnson could hear some heavy hammering below, along with some heavy language. Finally, the noise subsided and he heard Max say, "Mother of God!"

There was bundle after bundle of paper money in the room. All the bundles were brought up and put in the boat. Johnson then poured five gallons of fuel into the sub entrance and returned to the boat. At a distance of about a hundred feet, Max emptied his .45 at the entrance of the sub lid that was propped halfway up. Finally, a shot caused a spark and the fire was lit. Next, something happened that they hadn't expected. A large explosion, which set them all back a couple of feet.

Max and Johnson looked at each other and both wondered if the explosion of the sub's fuel tank or was the boat wired to do that. Max offered Johnson a drink, which was accepted.

Both of Myra's patients were now sitting up, on their own. Myra asked Max what happened to the side of his face and Max gave the same kind of answer he gave when she asked him what part of Camilla's body he had slapped. She knew he was lying and she was not having it.

Johnson grabbed Myra and showed her his bleeding fist. Before another question could be asked, they all turned to watch the sub slip below the water.

After a couple more drinks, Myra and the two men discussed what the next plan was to be.

Max explained that his orders were to bring the money to Ranger, if some was found, who would then turn it into the government in front of the press. They wanted the cartel to see the money was in the domain of the U.S. government.

Max admitted that the cartel might see through this plan and try to make examples of them. He mentioned that the cartel may not know of Johnson but he couldn't guarantee that. I could tell Ranger that there's no money. However, I do not believe this plan would cut the mustard with Ranger or the cartel. We also have these two girls to deal with. Both should be coming off their high soon. Does anyone else have any ideas?

Johnson said that his wife, Jane, would know where to take the two women for rehab. It wouldn't be cheap though.

Myra then offered a possible solution on what to do with them after two or three months of rehab. She suggested they could come to Sausalito and attend Pastor Ron's school. We would have to check with Ron, but being a minister, I do not think he would refuse them. Also, there may be legal issues in bringing the girls to the U.S.

Max suggested that Johnson take a small amount of the money to pay for rehab for the girls and maybe give $10,000 to the priest that found the 'baptismal certificate'.

Johnson thought that both ideas were good but said that they had to be careful. I can only imagine what the cartel or Ranger would do if they found out about this. He also suggested that they put a small amount of money in the walls of the C130 in case there were more expenses!

Max then said that he didn't want to hear anymore but reminded everyone not to get caught and that no good deed goes unpunished. If you are not comfortable with any of this, I will financially take care of it myself. Also, Johnson, talk this over with Jane before you do anything.

Max was now in a hurry to leave with the boat. He did not tell anyone that he saw a boat heading this way. He did not mention it to Johnson, but told Myra that she needed to go with him because one or both of the girls might go crazy when the drugs wore off. She could also help Jane get the girls to rehab. He told them that he would shut down his boat about fifty miles off of the coast of Peru and wait for Johnson to bring Myra back. He was reluctant to go into any port because of the bundled money on the boat.

Myra told Max that she agreed with his plan. She then went to the boat and grabbed a pair of jeans, a toothbrush, a blouse and some of the drug money, which she stuffed into her blouse. She then went to the plane.

Max helped Myra load up the two girls and then encouraged them to leave. He gave Myra a kiss and stuffed $20,000 down her blouse; only he was surprised to find money there already! He just smiled and ignored it. He complimented her on her figure.

Myra felt uneasiness in Max's kiss. Could it be that he was thinking of her sitting next to Johnson in a plane for two hours? She was still not over the Camilla incident.

Max went over the plan with Johnson. He would be waiting for them off the coast of Peru in about three days. He then encouraged them to leave again and was becoming angry at how slow they were going about it.

Johnson got the propeller spinning and the plane gracefully ascended into the air. The two girls looked excited and could not get over what was happening. They did not know English very well and no one had tried to explain to them what was taking place. Myra was concerned that Max had not given her a very good kiss. She soon figured out why when she saw a very fast boat approaching. She pointed it out to Johnson. She then turned to the back to get a better look and noticed the rifle lying on the seat; the one Johnson was bringing to Max. She told Max about the gun and Johnson said that he had meant to give it to Max. He told Myra to move the rifle up front.

Johnson told Myra to take the binoculars by her feet and see what she could see going on in the approaching boat. Myra reported that there were five men with rifles and one with a mounted machine gun. He then asked Myra if she knew how to use a rifle like that. She replied that Max had shown her how to shoot one very similar to that one. It's a .50 caliber and is going to bruise my shoulder! Johnson then told her to open the window and shoot down at the boat as he circled them. He also stressed the importance of not hitting the wing.

Myra missed with the first three shots and then didn't miss again. The shooters below didn't miss too often either. The .50 caliber bullets tore their fiberglass boat to shreds though. Soon there was smoke and then fire, and finally, an explosion.

It bothered Myra for a little while but soon she was over it when she thought about the two girls in the rear seats and what they must have gone through. The people on that boat were as disgusting as those Antifa crap weasels.

The girl sitting behind Myra saw all the shooting and tapped Myra on the shoulder and gave her a 'thumbs up'! She tapped Myra again and pointed to the blood coming form the leg of the other girl. Myra informed Johnson and went right to work on stopping the bleeding. Johnson gave her his belt to be used as a tourniquet. The girl was still pretty drugged up and didn't feel a thing.

The bullet had to travel through the wall of the plane to get to her leg. Myra informed Johnson of the situation and said that they would have to head for Valparaiso, but first they had to land the plane and put a couple cans of oil in the motor. Johnson didn't care if it ruined the engine; the oil pressure was dropping so fast he knew there was a leak. The temperature gauge was rising rapidly as well, which could mean a coolant leak.

The descent was smooth as was the water landing. Johnson located his oil and poured the oil into the reserve oil tank. He also checked for more damage and noticed the water hose had been hit. He found his electrical tape and tightly used the whole roll on the problem area. He knew the repair wouldn't last forever, but he figured it would get them to Valparaiso.

Myra was busy tending to the girl's wound. She was awake and complaining but seemed to understand what Myra was doing. Myra's probe for the bullet indicated that it was a shallow wound. The bullet was pretty well spent by the time it reached her leg. She extracted it with tweezers. She then cleaned up the wound with Mupirocin. Not knowing Spanish was probably a good thing during this process!

Soon they were in the air again. It stayed quiet all the way to Valparaiso. Johnson called ahead to the marina where Max and Myra had stayed and felt he could fix the plane there. He also called ahead to Jane to have her pick them up. He told Jane what size he thought the girls were because they were going to need some clothes.

Myra set about trying to determine the name of each girl. After much work, she found out the wounded girl's name was Willow, and the other girl's name was Ivy. Myra was glad to be finished with that task, only to be asked by Willow what everyone else's name was. The first one they wanted to know was for the big, tall man, then Myra and then the pilot. This was a process, but it did raise the spirits of the girls. Myra told Johnson that she felt more connected to them now.

Myra felt she was back home again as the plane floated up the dock. The marina manager was interested in the holes in the bottom of the plane. When he asked Myra about it, she just shrugged.

When Jane arrived, you could see the two women size each other up. It did not take long for the wall to come down and soon they were like old friends. The two women took Willow and Ivy into the marina and to the ladies' room and helped them dress. The clothes all fit well.

When they returned with the girls to the outside of the marina, Jane complimented Johnson on how well he had guessed their sizes. Johnson knew at the time it was a no-win assignment to guess the girl's sizes. He had not studied their bodies, as Jane would accuse him of later.

Myra suggested they go to the restaurant that her and Max had been to a number of times. Johnson had to carry Willow because of her leg wound. This was another no-win assignment. Willow soon fell asleep; it was touching. There wasn't going to be any homecoming love tonight for Johnson.

The bartender was happy to see Myra again. He asked Myra quietly if Max had beaten up those three guys. Myra told him that he might have and winked at him. Jane was eavesdropping. Myra gave the bartender the name of the priest she wanted to see. The bartender told her that he might not be able to do that because he has become a bit of a celebrity. Myra gave him Jane's address to give to the priest, hoping he could be there for breakfast in the morning. She also told him that she had a gift for the priest and the church.

The meal was great. Willow and Ivy really went to work on their food. Everyone felt them selves guarding their plate as they observed the two girls eating. Dessert was brought out for both of them for free.

Johnson picked up the tab and tipped the bartender $100, actually, to impress his wife and to pay for sins he did not commit. The walk back to the marina was downhill, which made it easier for Johnson to carry Willow. With her arm around his neck, she quickly fell asleep again. The little bitch just looked too comfortable! Johnson knew it was going to be a long drive home.

As they headed up to the marina, Myra noticed that it was going to be a pretty full car. She suggested to Jane that she could ride up front and they could get to know each other better. Jane had not driven more than ten feet when she stopped. She informed Myra that her husband was going to sit up front with her and Myra needed to ride in back with the girls. This was all right with Myra; she saw her mistake right away.

Johnson moved to the front and Myra went to the back. Johnson knew he was going to get punished again, even though he was just following orders!

Myra fell right to sleep, but the two girls did not, which made it impossible for Jane to discuss Johnson's behavior with the girls. She knew the girls were starting to pick up English and they were enjoying every word.

Jane's house was beautiful and it had four bedrooms but with three guests, she had some shuffling to do. Her children did not like to give up their rooms but her sixteen-year-old son saw someone he was willing to share his room with! Jane was all over that.

The night went quickly. Myra was the first to get dressed etc. She wanted to prepare herself for the meeting with the priest. She also packaged up $10,000 to give to the priest. Then she went to the kitchen and made some coffee. She was embarrassed at how clean Jane's kitchen was. Myra now wanted a house too, she was tired of sharing the marina with Ron and Peng. She also phoned Max, but there was no connection.

Back on the boat, Max was having some coffee. The ocean was smooth and he was making good progress. He tried to contact Ranger but he couldn't get a hold of him. Against his better judgments, he decided to contact Tracy. She answered on the first ring. Tracy was indifferent, hard to read. He reviewed with her the situation with Willow and Ivy. He let her know that Myra was talking to a priest about all this, the one that went to bat for Camilla. We are trying to learn about the girls and what the possible paths forward are. Note, we are not even sure what country of origin they have. We also gave the church some money for their help in all this.

Tracy asked where the money came from and Max's reply was that Myra was rich. He then politely ended the conversation before she started digging too much.

Max kept floating the idea in his head to open a bank account in every country he went past. He also remembered that he never closed his bank account on Omaha.

All the adults were in on the meeting with the priest, including Jane's son. The priest was in very good spirits, especially after receiving the $10,000 bundle. The priest said that he thought they should be able to locate the parents of Willow and Ivy. He felt they were most likely from Paraguay because of their accents. He brought up the fact that their parents might not even be alive or it could be that they had a falling out and don't wish to speak to them anymore. There is also the issue of Willow's mother, Mateo.

Myra explained that they all had empathy for Willow and Ivy and the best solution may be to move them to Sausalito, California. Myra made it clear that they were not going to just dump this problem off on Johnson and Jane. "When you come up with your findings, Max will come back down here. I would like to have Willow and Ivy in the meeting also, and in the meantime, is there a convent or secure proper facility for the girls near here. This would be too much work for Jane to house them here."

The meeting ended at this time and everyone seemed comfortable with the immediate plan.

Johnson contacted the marina to find the status on his airplane. He was told that it would be ready tomorrow.

Myra and Jane took the two girls shopping. The girls acted very mature and they had a fun day. They made out like bandits with all the clothes that were bought for them.

Myra told Jane that she did not think that the girls were addicted to drugs but that she should watch them closely for the next couple of days. This could have been their first trip with those bastards for all they knew. They were sex slaves or they were going to sell them somewhere. "Max and I will be home in approximately ten days and if there is an emergency, your husband has all of the contacts." Then Myra opened her purse and pulled out her Barretta and handed it to Jane, telling her to keep it in her purse and or next to her bed. "Your husband will show you how to use it. Hopefully you will never have to. The cartel is probably working overtime to find who all was involved. Hide the money well, they can use dogs to smell for it."

Tomorrow was going to be a big day for Myra and Jane. They were taking the two girls to a doctor to get physicals. After that, they were to be taken to a convent to stay until the priest figured out the best thing to do with them permanently. This plan was reviewed as best as was possible to the girls.

The evening went great. Johnson showed off his barbeque skills. They tried to keep the two girls involved with them. Their English seemed to improve by the hour. Everyone turned in early. Johnson waited until everyone was asleep and then quietly got out of bed and went to the hangar. He hid his cartel money in the C 130 and had not counted it; it turned out, he had grabbed $50,000!

At 8 AM the next day, the school bus came by and picked up the children. After the bus left, Johnson, Jane, Myra and the two girls drove to the marina in Valparaiso. At the marina, everyone said his or her good-byes. It was noticeable that the girls had bonded with Myra, which probably was caused because she was a nurse. Willow was quite proud of the wound on her leg that Myra had stitched shut.

Johnson and Myra went to the plane and checked it out. Everything looked proper but he also wanted four 5-gallon cans of fuel set in back of the plane.

The mechanic at the marina soon took care of the fuel. Johnson settled the bill and told the guy he didn't want to talk about the holes in the plane. They shook hands, each knowing they had just made a friend.

They taxied down the runway until it was wide enough for them to take off. Very quickly, they found themselves in the clouds.

Myra was a little nervous until they got above the clouds. In about an hour, Johnson phoned Max to get a better reading on his location.

Max told him that he could see the lights of Lima and that he was about fifty miles from the coast. He added that there was a small amount of rain coming down and the ceiling was about 200 feet.

Johnson was an experienced pilot. He slowly got below the clouds and sure enough, there was Max's boat.

The landing was very smooth. The plane was quickly secured to the boat, allowing Myra to make it safely to Max's arms. He gave his pregnant wife a very affectionate kiss.

Max and Johnson went right to work in putting fuel into the boats tank. Johnson said he would fly into Lima and refill the four 5-gallon cans and pick up some groceries and three dinner plates!

Now Max and Myra were alone again. She saw that there was some boat cleaning to do. She showed Max her bruised shoulder and told him all about what had happened to save his bacon. He thanked her for it and then scolded her for taking such a chance.

It took about two hours and then Johnson returned. He had his plane loaded up. He said that he figured Myra would be very hungry. Someone had told him that she was pregnant. She was a little embarrassed but at the same time, very proud to be in that condition.

The three of them sat down and quickly ate their meal. Max and Johnson set the cans of fuel on the boat. They next all went inside the boat to study the map as to the next drop. Johnson said that he was going to use the C 130 on the next trip and parachute the drop, which would contain a rubber inflatable boat to hold twelve cans of fuel. He said that it would be a little extra work but the water would be warm the next time they see each other. He felt the next meet point should be off the coast of El Salvador.

Johnson had a smooth takeoff. It got rough when he entered the clouds. The trouble that day though, was that the clouds got heavy very fast. He did something a good pilot never does; he did not study the weather report before he took off. He knew Max and Myra were in for it. He tried to call Max but he couldn't make contact. He then tried for the airport at Santiago and he got through. They informed him that the ceiling was at 100 feet and the clouds went up to 30,000 feet. They did not think there would be a break for at least four hours. He next contacted the airport at Conception and they said it was all clear. He had enough to get to Conception but if it cleared up over Santiago that would be great.

Max and Myra were now in heavy seas. They were both concerned. He remembered, someone telling him to avoid having a big wave hit you on the side, you could get swamped. Myra checked everywhere for leaks and found none. They were now becoming confident that everything was okay. After four hours the storm let up. The sea was still rough but the danger of being swamped was over.

Max told Myra to see if she could get some sleep. She tried for a while but claimed that she couldn't sleep in a storm.

The sunset and in about two hours they had a moon. The ocean calmed and, in the distance, they could see the lights of Lima. Max decided that they were too close to shore and changed their direction to northwest.

Johnson made it home at midnight. He had to fly all the way to Conception. It was not enjoyable flying and he was physically drained when he landed and finally shut the plane down. Jane was happy to see him. He informed Jane that Myra was pregnant. Jane immediately asked whom he had heard that from. He told her that he was just guessing and Myra fell for it.

Jane told her husband," It sounds to me like you are studying women again and I suppose you know what size bra she wears too!"

Johnson was tired and upset with the question and said with a smile, "She wasn't wearing one." He slept on the couch.

In the morning, Jane had breakfast ready for her husband. She was kind of ashamed of herself and she even brought him coffee. She also told him that she had something else for him after the bus picked up the kids.

She informed her husband that the girls were at a convent and she wanted to bring them over for a day on the weekend. She didn't want the girls to think they'd just been dumped there.

"How old is Willow?" their son, Gregg, asked.

He received a stare from Myra that could have cut glass. Gregg was too much like his father. Johnson took a lot of heat for this and Jane told her husband to have that "father/son talk" he was supposed to have had many times since the boy had turned sixteen!

Chapter 16

LOS CABOS

After three days, Max and Myra were about 100 miles off the coast of El Salvador. The weather was fine and they figured that in about an hour, the C -130 should be flying over them. Max called Johnson and told him where he thought they were. Just when Max started to worry, the C 130 came out of the clouds and scared the hell out of them. Johnson flew about 50 feet from the boat. He laughed the whole time, thinking how Max was an expert at a lot of things that he couldn't do, but he couldn't fly! He ascended to about 200 feet and then parachuted the cans of fuel and the deflated rubber boat. Then he showed off a bit and left.

Max put on a life jacket, grabbed a rope and swam over to the deflated raft. He pulled the rip -cord and before he knew it, there was a boat in front of him. He then swam back to the boat and grabbed another rope he had tied to the boat and started attaching the rope to the nearest three cans. He continued this process until all the fuel cans were secured to the boat. He then got back on board the boat and put his clothes on. He pulled the raft next to the rear of the boat and retied the rope. The next step was basic, pull the cans up to the inflatable raft and load them on. Periodically, he would organize the containers and tie them down. He stopped with twelve cans. The remaining four cans went directly into his boat's tanks.

He did not allow Myra to handle the heavy cans due to her 'condition'. He then had a PBR, but did to allow her to have one, because of her 'condition'.

Myra and Max made steady progress heading almost due north. The weather was great. They only problem they had were a dwindling food supply.

Their fuel supply dropped to dangerous levels by the time they got to the same latitude as the top of Mexico. Max had no choice but to call the Ranger, however, he could not be reached. Eventually, a call back was made by his military secretary/answering service. She informed Max that Ranger had been redeployed to Afghanistan, and in the future to refer to him as 'General'.

Max's next call was to Tracy. He spoke Farsi to her. She replied back in English, saying that they could now speak English because the money they found belonged to 'us', since it was found on the high seas and not in any country's territorial water.

Max continued to talk in Farsi, saying he was going to drop anchor in the bay off of Los Cabos. "Get yourself a private flight down here so we can talk. Hopefully, a fuel boat can come here and fill my tank. If they do not have that service, you will have to figure out a way to get me fuel. I don't want to check in with customs, etc. Oh, and bring Myra a plate of food."

Tracy told him that she would be down there in a few hours and said not to get too close to the port. "We have come too far to lose the 'cargo' now!"

Myra and Max changed course to Los Cabos. He hoped that he did not come too close to the port, however, if the water were too deep, he wouldn't be able to anchor.

Tracy had a boyfriend of sorts, who had a plane, but she didn't want to get another person involved. She felt that they were already dividing that money up in enough ways. She finally found a private service that could leave within the hour. She hurriedly went to her apartment and grabbed some clothes and then made for the airport.

The pilot was ready. There were no creature comforts on the plane. No map was to be taken and the pilot carried on a conversation the whole time. She finally, as politely as she could, told him to 'Shut the fuck up!" He flew close to the ground the rest of the way, just to annoy her. No tip was given. Right after she got off of the plane, she heard the word, 'bitch'.

Tracy had to hoof it to the port facilities. She found a fueling boat. She contacted Max, who was anchored in the bay. She rode along with the fueling boat to Max's boat.

Max had the boat fueled and all the extra fuel cans filled. They were now ready to shove off, except there was no plate of food for Myra!

Tracy and Myra rode back with the fuel boat. They were back in about an hour with three plates of the best Mexican food in the world. They ate and then sailed into the sunset.

Max said that he would handle the boat while Myra and Tracy counted and sorted the money into $50,000 bundles. He also told them that he planned on shutting down at Santa Catalina Island. He felt he should be able to anchor there and get five or six hours of sleep. He planned to sleep in the wheel- house.

Myra planned on checking on Max throughout the night. Tracy said she would too. If anyone saw anything strange, everyone was to be awoken.

At 2 am, they reached Catalina Island. They dropped anchor in the bay so as to not get involved with any activity on the dock. Max grabbed a blanket and went right to sleep.

About two hours later a boat came towards them from the direction of the dock. Tracy was in the boat and checked her hand cannon to make sure it was loaded. She also kicked Max's foot, quickly waking him. Max turned all lights on and alerted Myra. The boat approaching changed course and headed for the open sea.

This activity bothered Max and he had Tracy make some coffee. Max still needed more sleep. Tracy brought Max some coffee and told him that there was around 50 million dollars on the boat. She told Max to get some more sleep and she would stay on guard. At about that time, Myra came up to stay on guard also.

Max got his beauty sleep while Myra guided the boat north. She noticed that there were more lights on the coast. The country was recovering.

Myra and Max figured they would be home around midnight. There were no weather factors to delay them. There was a boat going in the same direction as theirs, however, it could be a coincidence. They were at least five miles behind. They were too far away for binoculars to identify what type a boat it was.

Probably because she was pregnant, Myra wanted a house. There was a well-kept, older house up the block from the marina that was for sale. Even with the plague, it was still expensive. It looked like it had four bedrooms. They certainly had the money to purchase it, but a cash sale would certainly cause some problems with the IRS. Myra was planning on talking to an accountant on the matter.

Tracy told Myra that her run for mayor of San Diego fell through. Her opponent was dredging up too much dirt on her. She had heard about an upscale restaurant near the marina that interested her. Tracy felt that money would be no problem for her now, but worried that paying with cash would be a red flag. She too, needed to talk to an accountant.

Max was the first one to see the Golden Gate Bridge in the distance. He pointed it out to Myra. They both knew that this would be their final home.

When they got back to the marina, Ron and Peng came running out to see them. Fred, Camilla and Andrew soon arrived as well.

Fred pointed out that there were three more shops opening up back on the boardwalk. He told him that this place was going to be booming in another year.

Camilla drew everyone's attention by telling what she was doing in Fred's house. She was painting, decoration a room for the baby. She was also wearing a hatching jacket, even though there was no need to do that yet.

Myra felt the oxygen leaving her side of the room again. She just shrugged it off and hoped only the best for her and Andrew.

Max was the first to notice that Matt was missing. Ron took Max away from the group and showed him a piece of paper with a hand-written message on it saying, "$100,000 if you want to see your son again. Bring the money to the south entrance of the Golden Gate Bridge on Thursday. Put it into the back of a red pickup. Your son will be allowed to come home later in the day."

Max took the message and went to his and Myra's room, where he could think and plan. He soon called Peng into the room. He asked to see all of Matt's schoolwork and asked her if she knew if he had a girlfriend. He told her to check the laundry for clues. Now wasn't the time to be bashful.

Peng soon returned with a few books and a notebook and a garment with lipstick on it. Peng muttered something in Mandarin. Tracy picked it up and rolled her eyes. Peng found a small picture of an African American girl with the name Maxine on the back of it.

Max handed the picture to Fred and told him that there was a photo store down the block and he wanted the photo duplicated three hundred times and to hurry!

Next, Max grilled Andrew and Camilla. He figured that brothers talk to each other and so do girlfriends, when they are together.

Andrew said that he had met her once when Matt was out with her. She was concerned if Matt's mother would like her. She seemed very smart and always had one hand on Matt. I think, from what I saw, that they were close. Anyway, Camilla talked with her more than I did.

Camilla was now on the hot seat. She was a little scared of Max and his abrasive tone wasn't helping. She told him that it was just girl talk about her job at the bakery.

Max cut her off, "What bakery?"

Camilla said, "The one by the Bay Bridge."

Max calmly thanked her and said, "We've just got our first lead!" He then addressed Ron, asking him to take his daughter-in-law to the Bay Bridge and find that bakery and talk to the employees calmly and ask them if she is out with Ron's son, etc. He also told Ron that he was asking him to do this because Ron knew the city better than any of the rest of them. Call us on your cell phone. We will most likely be somewhere around Berkeley.

Max then tried to reach Ranger by calling his wife. She answered and said, "I have been trying to get a hold of you. My husband, who is actually a General, now, is in trouble again. He is pinned down behind enemy lines. He says he can hold out for about a week. He says that you have particular knowledge of the mountain where he is pinned down."

Max told her of the problem at hand that he had to take care of first, but that he hoped to take care of it today. What he needed to accomplish this was a file Ranger had kept on Matt.

She said that she had the file and had meant to send it to Sausalito but hadn't gotten around to it. I will send it to you by one of these privates who have nothing to do. It should be there in less than an hour. She ended the conversation by saying, "My husband depends on you, so be careful."

It took one hour exactly for the file to make it Sausalito. In the meantime, they moved all the bundles from the boat to a secure room in the marina.

Fred, Tracy and Peng were considered the absolute firewall in protecting the money while the locating and freeing of Matt was taking place. Note also that there was a police force operating in Sausalito now but getting the police involved in protecting the money wasn't something that anybody brought up. Max made sure that Fred, Tracy and Peng were well armed. Max felt comfortable leaving Tracy behind, knowing she would never give up any money. This was her last chance of getting rich.

Max read through the file, which said the following:

"Antifa maintained a headquarters, in a closed church in Oakland, close to the Oakland Bay Bridge. The church doors are boarded up except for a rear door that still operated with a key. There was no alarm system or electrical power. There was a electrical cable running from a nearby, unoccupied house. This is a poor part of the city and most of the homes had been condemned. Only one room was used in the church and that was in the basement."

Max read this to the group. He informed them that Matt was working undercover to find out where their money was coming form. He also told them about Maxine, but it did not say if she was involved. They already knew that Camilla and Ron were somewhere near this church trying to find out anything about Maxine.

Max told the group that they would head out now in two cars. My Jeep will be one of the cars. It should take us about an hour to get there and the sun will be setting around then. We will drive by the church property one time for a look-see of the area. We will then park and burst through the door. Note that it does work on a lock and maybe they will be careless and we can just walk on in. And, first of all, I am trained on matters like this so I will go first. It is my belief that these are a bunch of amateurs and are just after some easy money. If possible, we will not kill anyone but they will get an education.

Max slipped a sledgehammer into the Jeep. He made sure everyone had a weapon. Then they immediately took off for the Oakland Bay Bridge. It was Sunday and the traffic was light. Everyone was excited and scared and worried about Matt.

They drove by the church as planned. Everything looked quiet. Max phoned Ron to let him know where they were. Max reminded everyone to be careful with there guns and to only use them when necessary.

Everyone got out of the cars. Max pulled his hickory stick out of the Jeep and put his .45 in the other hand. He had not used the stick since Omaha. He planned on using it now!

Max checked the door and found it to be locked. He told everyone to backup up and then shot the lock at close range with his .45. The shot was noisy and scared the hell out of everyone. Max bolted through the door. The light was on in a room down the hall. He ran to the room and was met by six Antifa thugs, both men and women. One of them had a gun and Max had to dispatch him as he took aim. The rest of the despicable group immediately turned into cowards, huddling together in the rear of the room.

Matt was tied to a chair. His head was tilted forward. They had beaten him considerably. Max had no mercy now. As the others guarded the group at the back of the room, Myra and Andrew freed Matt and carried him to the back of the Jeep.

Max then took each person from the back of the room into the hallway and beat them severely. He knew how to beat someone without killing the person. The scars would remain the rest of their lives. No one was moving when Max left the church!

Myra knew it would be best to take Matt to an emergency room but they would surely ask questions. It could be a real mess with the police considering that Max had killed one of them. They decided to take Matt home. Myra called Ron and let him know what had happened and what was still going on. Ron was very upset and was not as forgiving as a person of the cloth should be. He told her that they had Maxine with them in case she needed to be interrogated more.

Matt was conscious when they arrived at the marina. He was not saying much and appeared to be lost. He asked for his dad and his mother and Maxine. Matt's parents wanted to know more about Maxine before they gave her their blessing. Matt's file made no derogatory comments about her.

Camilla and Andrew stayed very close to each other. They did not want their world turned upside down. Camilla also went and gave Fred a hug. With what she saw that day, she would always feel better, especially at night, with old man Fred and his shotgun in the house.

Myra worked on Matt for most of the night. If the cuts were not treated immediately and correctly, he could end up with ugly scars. His nose was broken. She asked Peng to hold his head but she would start screaming every time Myra tried to set it straight. Maxine was watching and came over with a powerful grip. Myra got it set straight on the first try. She did not flinch with all the blood either. Matt seemed to find some peace with Maxine holding his hand. She stayed and helped Myra through the night.

Myra was too busy working on Matt and Max needed to talk to someone about the money, so by default, he sat down and talked to Tracy. He told Tracy that he felt that they needed to get the money out of there. He wanted $50,000 bundles put into safe deposit boxes throughout San Francisco and Los Angeles. He wanted them set up with both your name and Myra's name on them. In other words, both of you would need to sign to open the box.

Max continued by explaining we will still have too much money in the marina. We could also buy a safe, but that is almost advertising that we have money. He went on to tell Tracy that he was flying to Afghanistan tomorrow. My friend and the man I frequently work for are trapped on a mountain near Kandahar. He said that he was fairly confident he could spring the trap but sometimes shit happens. We need adults in the room when decisions are made about the money. He told her that he was leaving behind a list of people who are connected in one way or another to the money. This list should be a good starting point for decisions that might have to be made. If we fight over the money, everything will fall apart. Note also, we may have to deal with the Cartel too. In conclusion, when I talk to Myra in a couple days on the phone, I would like to have an idea of what you come up with. Note, we could easily get robbed. We have to hurry up and move on this. Also, if this is going to take some time, have Fred put a steel door on our money room. The more I think of that, the more I like it.

Max went back over to Myra and told her that he had to fly out in the morning. He explained the situation as best as he could. However, he did not mention Afghanistan.

Myra told him that she would be working most of the night on Matt and she felt that they needed the doors locked and at least two people with guns on guard at all times.

Max said that he had talked with Tracy on much of these same matters. I will be talking on the phone with you in two days. He gave her a kiss and then went and locked all the doors. He also told Fred that he would like him and Andrew and Camilla to move back into the marina until he got back. And bring your shotgun!

Max went to bed. He had no problems sleeping, because he felt this group would stick together.

Chapter 17

KANDAHAR

In the morning, Max woke up at seven and packed. By eight, he was ready to go. He woke Myra and gave her a kiss. She told him to retire after this job; I want to grow old with you! Also, your baby is starting to kick.

Max had a hard time leaving. He flew out of San Francisco, first class. He needed more sleep and free beer. The lady sitting next to him tried to strike up conversation and he had to tell her that he hadn't slept in two days and he just couldn't talk right now. She turned and looked the other way!

He had to switch planes twice to get there, but he arrived well rested. He went straight to military headquarters, which were expecting him. He was given a uniform and any weapon he wanted. He said that he had a .45 in his luggage but would like an M-14 with a scope, if they still stock that relic.

They still stocked the M-14 but it didn't have a scope. He said that was okay, he was too slow with a scope anyway. He was issued several boxes of ammunition for the M-14 and for his .45. He got on the next convoy to Kandahar.

At Kandahar, to his surprise, he ran into Johnson. It felt really great to have a beer with him. Jane wanted him to retire too. He told Max; that the situation here didn't sit well with him, too many soldiers are dying. We have to get this mountain back! Johnson explained to Max he had a plan, but he couldn't sell it to the General.

Max grabbed a couple more beers and wanted to know what the plan was. Johnson got out a topo map of the area in question. He said you can see our troops basically have the high ground but are also surrounded. Note that the last 50 yards to the top are too rugged for a chopper to land on. And, if the chopper attempts to land or lower troops, it becomes a target. We have already lost a number of troops trying that. The backside of the mountain is too steep to climb. We are 300 yards from breaking through. We can do it but we will lose a lot of soldiers in the process. My plan is to make a major build up of troops and tanks in the middle section of the battle line. The night before, you would take that unit of ROK troops that just arrived from South Korea up the left side. These ROK troops have a well-earned reputation for being nasty little bastards. These troops are very well trained to crawl on the ground to achieve their objective without being seen or heard. In addition, I want those soldiers to be equipped with the AR-15, which will spit a tremendous number of bullets in a short period of time. The area will be showered with bullets. Hopefully, they will not expect the main thrust will be coming from the left. There will also be a feint attack from the right. The large build-up in the middle will make a lot of noise and mainly shoot low so they do not shoot our troops on the other side. We don't want you to shoot too high and kill Ranger's troops 300 yards away. This will be tricky business and we will not be able to practice. Also, I don't want anybody to go over this plan with the troops until we are well outside the fort. That includes our cell phones!

Max liked the plan and told Johnson to present it to the General again.

Johnson said it would be better if we both went in there and talked to the General and his staff. You have quite a reputation and that may sell the plan.

They both went to the General's office to sell the plan. The General said that he was busy now with his staff so he wanted to get on with it. Max saluted the general and said that he didn't want to get started until the cleaning lady left the room, actually the building. The General assured him that she could be trusted. Max gruffly said that it was his ass on the line and reminded him of the many problems with leaks they'd had in the last six months.

The General knew he had no other card to play so he agreed.

Max and Johnson then left the General's office. Johnson wanted to review his plan so there would be a smooth presentation. And Max wanted get another beer and see if he could locate this trooper from the 10th Mountain Division that Johnson told him about. Johnson had told him he would most likely be in the compounds bar.

Max went straight to the bar and sure enough, there sat a young trooper from the 10th Mountain Division. He went straight over to the trooper and sat down. And after introducing himself he said I guess you are Mike. At first Mike paid not attention to Max, but when he felt a heavy hand on his drinking wrist and figured he would have to carry on a conversation with the bastard. He replied that he was Mike.

Max informed him that he had a job for him to do. And Mike replied in a slurred voice that he was not interested! That was not the right reply and Max told the barkeep to not allow anyone to follow him and Mike outside. He also told the barkeep that he worked directly for the General.

The barkeep was savvy enough to understand the situation and also wanted this drunk out of his bar. Max had at least 50 pounds on Mike and easily escorted him outside to the rear of the building. He then asked Mike why he was drinking all the time. He did not readily reply, but did let go with a haymaker, which missed its target! This action found Mike slammed several times against the wall again. Mike was now ready to talk. He said he lost his entire family to the plague and wanted to die. He also said that some damn General that knew his family sent me to this godforsaken place. He was one of them do-gooders that can't seem to mind their own business!

Max informed Mike that before he dies, he has a job to do for him. He went on to say that it appears you are the only one at this entire Fort that has the skill to do it. You are going to climb that big fucking mountain to the west of us when it gets dark tonight. You are going to get a chance to redeem yourself by relaying an important message to an embattled group of soldiers at the top that are about to be overrun. If I had someone else to do it, I would use someone else. I am not sure a drunk can do the job. The General that sent you here thinks you have the right stuff. Someone with a higher pay-grade them me has given you another chance to redeem yourself. Don't fuck it up!

At this point Mike began to puke. When he finally paused, he slurred out, "I can do it"!

Max felt good about the reply and ushered Mike to the shower building. Inside, he commandeered a low ranking soldier to keep Mike in the shower for two hours. He also commandeered another hapless soldier to go to Mike's quarters and retrieve another uniform and a jacket. He also gave both of the commandeered soldiers an order that they will get him into a clean uniform and make him ready for a difficult assignment in about three hours. If he is not ready, both of you will be climbing a mountain in the dark tonight! If someone of importance comes along and wants to know what you are doing, just tell them you are doing a job for Max and Ranger. Tell them to go and see the General if they have a problem with that.

Both of the commandeered soldiers were good-sized guys and they were not stupid. One look at Max told them; this is someone important and climbing a mountain in the dark is not for them!

When the General was finally ready, Max and Johnson took turns giving the presentation, each covering their area of expertise. Surprisingly, the General gave them the okay and asked them when they wanted to do it.

Max had now mostly taken over and said that it would take ten hours to get up the left side of the mountain and he wanted to start as soon as it was dark, also noting that there was no moon tonight. In conclusion, I understand you have a soldier here from the 10th Mountain Division, by the name of Mike. I would like to have him delivered to the backside of the mountain to climb and verbally deliver the plan to our forces up there.

The General said Mike was a good man, but he drinks! You will have to check on his condition. The General said, the 10th Mountain Division General that sent him here believes this soldier can be developed, and as you know, with the plague and all, it is very hard to find any good soldiers.

Johnson told the General that he would check his condition. Also, I need someone in a chopper to bring him to the base of the mountain on the backside when it gets dark. By the time he gets to the top of the mountain, he will be sober. This may be the most important link in the operation. We are confident he can do the job.

Max requested one of the General's staff introduce Johnson and me to the ROK troops, and we will need 50 troops. If there are more available, keep them at the base of the mountain in case some of the enemy tries to escape. This will put fear into them if none escape. Also, we will not make a move against the enemy until you, pointing at Johnson, start attacking from the middle. Note that once we are all in place, we will have the enemy completely surrounded.

The General then addressed Max, saying, "you will have a female reporter with you. She is with the New York Times."

Max was not happy with this news, but he respectfully told the General that she needed to see him within the hour.

After Max left the office, and in a secluded area, he told Johnson that he wanted six men to scatter out in the desert, outside the walls and remain there all night. I suspect we will catch a spy leaving the fort. If we catch one, make sure to take him/her alive. We are going to get him/her to sing.

Max's meeting with April, the reporter, did not go smooth. He started by telling her that she would not know where they were going or the timetable. It is up to you to keep up with us. We will not carry you. If at any time, you slow us down, I will send you back and I surely wouldn't want to be alone at night in a desert full of Arabs. It is imperative that you remain quiet at all times. The Korean soldiers we will be with have been trained to be quiet. There will be no cell phones. If your cell phone goes off, I will immediately destroy it. Bring your own water and coat; the desert gets cold at night. We leave in fifteen minutes.

April asked no questions.

The general's staff officer arrived with an NCO from the ROK troops. He was introduced to Byung-ho, the highest -ranking NCO from the company of troops. There were no officers. Max gave him a cordial greeting. Max was brief and said that they would stop in two hours, when they were well away from the fort, and he would brief him and his second in command exactly what they were going to do. We will march in a column of twos. Also, make sure they are all wearing a vest and a coat. Make sure everyone has at least 500 rounds and two grenades. We will be leaving in half an hour. They should also carry water and food. Keep your food and water hidden from sight.

Max carried two jugs of water and four candy bars along with his .45 and M-14 rifle.

Buyng-ho led the column into the desert towards the mountain. Max walked alongside the column, making sure that all the soldiers were ok, etc. April was the last person in the column. Max moved her up to the middle. After two hours, he signaled Buyng-ho to stop the column.

Max had him bring him 10 soldiers at a time and the two of them went over the plan. Emphasis was on bringing to their attention that care must be placed as to where they were aiming. If you aim too high or too far to the left or too far to the right, you could hit our own troops. Also, stay in a tight unit so we do not hit one another. There should be a considerable number of flares overhead. We have to push them hard to the middle where the big guns will destroy them.

After reviewing the plan with the last group, Buyng-ho started the column towards the mountain. Soon, the path started to go uphill. Grumbling was heard now and again. Every hour the column stopped for fifteen minutes.

Approximately at this same time, it was getting dark and a chopper landed at the Fort to pick up Mike. The two commandeered soldiers helped Mike get into the chopper and then one of the soldiers shook his hand, looking him in the eye, told him, "you weren't picked for this job unless someone knew you could do it. I will be praying for you".

The chopper pilot was cocky, like most of the others in his unit. He gave the impression that with this chopper he could do anything and make it back alive. He told Mike to hang on because we will be coming in low with the lights off and there is no moon.

Immediately they were airborne and Mike was getting the puking feeling again. He was able to forgo it. He was hanging on for his dear life and could see very little outside. He noticed the pilot had a cigar in his mouth and was very intent on what he was doing. He did manage to say his name was Rooster and he had never been shot down. And in a cocky way, he said he was the best chopper pilot there ever was.

It took the chopper about an hour to get to the drop-off location. Just as the chopper touched down, Mike could hear several bullets making contact and Mike's heart was doing double time! Rooster yelled back to Mike to jump out and run for the mountain and get at least a hundred feet up, because everything below that point was going to get raked until he ran out of bullets.

Mike hit the ground running and never looked back. He could hear the bullets raking the desert below, which encouraged him to climb even faster. And then the explosion! The desert was briefly lit up. Mike knew Rooster could have never survived and wondered if them bastards would be coming after him next. He figured they would have to be able to see in the dark and be very good climbers to do so!

Mike's efforts to make it to the top were beyond anything he had attempted before. At one point in desperation, he removed his jacket to reduce his weight and give himself more room to maneuver. Occasionally he would hear machinegun fire splattering the wall he was climbing, but nowhere near his position. In another act of desperation he blindly jumped from one location to another. When his hand found a firm grip during this jump in the dark, he knew he was not alone and would make it to the top!

Back with the ROK soldiers, April did not look to be in good shape. Max took a look to see what her condition was like. He found that she was carrying a backpack with several large books and extra water. Max put the backpack next to a rock and carried the extra water. He then took her shoes off and noticed that she wasn't wearing any socks. One of the other soldiers saw this and threw her a clean pair of socks. April was crying quietly. What had she gotten herself into? She thought this would be an interesting assignment and now she might die.

Max bent down and told her not to let anyone see her cry. He then told her to hurry up and catch up with the rest. To get her moving faster, he told her that enemy scouts were probably watching them and if they found her, they would probably rape her and cut her throat! Her pace picked up immediately. Max gave her a candy bar to get her energy level up.

Max told Byung-ho to send scouts ahead. He did not want to walk in to a trap. He was starting to worry if they were making enough progress. It was so dark that it was hard to determine where they were. A flare went off high above him and gave him the view he needed.

Byung-ho stopped the troops for another break. While on the break, one of the scouts returned, saying that he had met up with some of the troops that came up with Johnson. He determined that they had two more hours until sunrise.

Byung-ho got the column moving. Another soldier handed his rifle to his buddy and reached down and snatched up April. This guy was a solid brute that you would never want to spill a beer on. April felt ashamed but she did not have the energy to continue!

Max took two of the ROK soldiers up the hill. In the darkness, they ran into four enemy scouts. A quick knife fight ensued. We lost one and they lost four.

Now Max went on alone. The other scout stayed with the dead soldier and waited for the column to arrive. When the column saw one of there own, they were very upset and ready for anything that came their way. April took some pictures and after reviewing the mess, was ready and able to walk on her own.

When Max returned, he pointed out the sheer rocks to the left and all the way forward. Another scout came there way in the dark and they almost killed him. Everybody was getting very edgy.

The scout was Mike from the 10th Mountain Division. He quickly remarked that they did not look very friendly and what were all those dead enemy soldiers lying around?

Max then noticed that Mike's hands were bleeding and asked him how that had happened. He said he was halfway up the mountain last night and could not see. I was hanging on with one hand for about ten minutes when I asked for help. I then felt my grip slipping and I jumped and slid down about twenty feet and found the perfect path. I promised never to drink again!

Max said he was glad to hear that his pledge was heard. If I ever see a drink in your hand you will be in for a quality beating!

Max reviewed the area with Byung-ho. He pointed out the sheer rocks on the left and the broad path before them. He felt they had another five thousand feet and then they would run into the enemy. He ordered Mike, and Byung-ho to build a defensive position there, in case the enemies made a big push on the left.

Mike and Byung-ho got the defensive position squared up. The ROK troops were working at a feverish pitch. This would be there first taste of battle, everyone had something to prove.

Mike came up to Max and said that he knew a pathway alongside the sheer wall to pull out the 'lost battalion'. He and the ROK troops could get through to them and lead them out. Once they were out, Johnson could turn his howitzers on the whole area without fear of killing our own soldiers.

Max told him that he had better know what he was capable of, but Byung-ho needed to stay with his own troops. This area is the only way out for the enemy once the howitzers open up. You are going to Ranger's position. And don't ever call his men the 'lost battalion'; he will put you on shit duty for a year!

Byung-ho got his orders and Mike and Max took off with ten ROK troops. They went as fast as was safe, the sun was about to rise! It took half an hour to get there. The entire area was in chaos because Johnson's unit was dropping in mortar rounds with pinpoint precision.

Ranger's comment when Max arrived was, "Where the hell have you been?" There were fifty soldiers to move and half were injured. Mike, working with one of Rangers soldiers, got the group moving. Max called Johnson and told him to chew the entire area up in ten minutes with every weapon he had and, I believe they will try escaping to the left. Also, don't send anyone into the battlefield; let the big guns do their job!

It was a big and dangerous task for Max and the ROK soldiers to get the wounded out of there. They were all aware that the big guns were going to pulverize the area in about twenty minutes. It was also starting to get light out. Max called Johnson to see if smoke shells could be lobbed in. And if the enemy soldiers were spotted, there would be casualties.

To add to Max's problems, there was the female reporter that had somehow followed them. She was taking pictures as fast as she could.

Max yelled to April and pointed to a stretcher being carried by two men. He told her to walk along the side of the stretcher and hold his hand and encourage him not to give up! The wounded man's hand was all bloody. She took a deep breath and did what she was told. She aged several years in the walk back.

More ROK soldiers ran up the trail to help Ranger's men get to safety. The wounded were moved far behind the defensive line to make sure stray bullets didn't hit them. All of Ranger's men that were not wounded found a place in the line.

Max did not figure the enemy would surrender. In his mind, they deserved to die. He had seen what they had done to his wounded and the troops that had surrendered. He was going to give them a taste of his justice. There was the Army way and then there was Max's way!

Max grabbed April by her arm and told her that the enemy would have to kill them to escape and they wouldn't be taking prisoners. They may take you alive, but you won't be going to a prison. Find a place to hide and do whatever it takes to survive or die trying!

The next time Max saw April, she was behind a log with a rifle next to her and she had stopped taking pictures. She knew her employer would twist whatever he saw in her pictures anyway!

As Max had predicted, the enemy made their final attempt to win the battle. They were screaming Allah Akbar!

Byung-ho did not wait for the enemy to make it to the line, he and his men charged directly at them. This move even surprised Max. This was their first blood and he did not think they would be up for it. The fighting was a 'kill or be killed' situation. There would be no retreat for either side. Max went to work with his .45. It was his weapon of choice at close range. The fighting lasted almost a half hour. Some of the soldiers on both sides died because they were too exhausted to defend themselves.

In the end, there were no enemy soldiers left alive. He counted twenty dead ROK soldiers, including Byung-ho. He found April with a big knife in her leg that she couldn't pull out. Mike was found shot in the leg but he would live. Ranger was found dead! It would have to be a closed casket!

Max was without a wound that showed. His wound was remembering those that died and dreading the call to their loved ones.

The choppers with medical teams soon arrived. There were over 200 enemy dead at the "left" battlefield and over 500 dead due to artillery in the "middle" battlefield. This was a big loss for the enemy.

It appeared that April had killed the enemy soldier that had stabbed her. She blew his brains out at close range. When the medic tried to tend to her wound, she demanded that they clean the bits of brain off of her first! The medic complained about her language. Max had a brief conversation with Mike. He felt sorry for him getting shot in the leg and so he told him that he would be up for a high-level medal. For Max, there would be no medal; he was not technically in the military. He was a soldier for hire or a soldier of fortune and his employer had just died!

All of the ROK soldiers received a ride back in the choppers. Most of the soldiers in Johnson's group would be there for some time processing and accounting for the dead.

This particular mountain had caused the military many problems. It was important because of its location and in the not too distant future, it would become an outpost for the military.

Much to the chagrin of the General back at the Fort, a spy was caught leaving in the desert. This spy took some convincing, but eventually she sang like a bird. Rather than executing her at the Fort, she was turned loose about 200 miles into the desert!

Johnson's performance during the battle was given high praise. A request was made by the Fort General to have him transferred to the Army. Johnson refused the transfer. He planned to retire from the Air Force in two years.

Max was considered the key to the success of the battle, however, there was an abhorrent number of enemy soldiers who had died from a .45 to the head at close range. Max was becoming a "hot potato". This accusation did not bother Max; he would be hired again, and most likely by the same people who condemned him now. As soon as there was a situation that required his expertise.

Mike's wound was extensive, and would require many months for recovery. He flew back in the same plane as April. She wanted to do a lengthy story on him and his unique experience in the Army and his conversion to Christianity.

Max stayed at the Fort for a few days calling the loved ones of those who had died.

Each of the General's staff were required to spend at least two hours each with Max, just to learn things, etc. that aren't taught in military manuals.

Max finally found time at night, which would be day in Sausalito, to talk to Myra. She intently listened to his lies and just thanked God that he was okay. Max always knew how to change the subject from battle to, 'has my daughter been kicking a lot?'

Max said he did give a lot of thought to getting a steel safe-like door on the money room. He now liked the idea. He wanted Myra to think about Tracy managing the money and having himself and Myra acting as oversight. Tracy would submit a report every quarter on the financial affairs. He also told her that he wanted to triple the size of the marina. He wanted a better view of San Francisco and the Golden Gate Bridge. Also, we should consider the private school Ron keeps talking about starting.

Max then got emotional and said, "Ranger is dead!" There was some silence and then he assured Myra that he was going to retire from being a "soldier-for-hire".

Myra knew the two statements were tied together. There was some more silence and then Max said, "Ranger was a better man than me. I have seen the elephant in the room"! He went on to say that he wanted to spend time helping raise their daughter, learning how to be an expert sailor, and work with Matt researching the present conspiracy theory we have been kicking around for some time now. This research would include the following:

1. Sightings of George Soros called into the KMR News in New York City. (Matt has a cousin working there)
2. Locate the source of the Red Pill. (Believed to be in the Amazon)
3. Who finances Antifa?
4. Who developed the plague?
5. Determine what happened to the Nazi gold brought in by U-boats to some location in the Amazon.
6. Prove or disprove that the plague was created to cause an unimaginable crises to enable the Globalist and or Socialists to take over the world.

This project would require a number of trips to South America. And with the money we now have we may buy a second home somewhere over there.

Max ended the conversation by telling Myra that there would still be time on his schedule to give her some much-needed attention!

Chapter 18

The 4th of July

It was the 4th of July in Sausalito and Reverend Ron and his wife Peng put on a party on a newly constructed parking lot behind the marina. Invitations had been sent out two weeks ago to the following guests, Max and Myra, Johnson and Jane, Ivy and Willow, Fred, Tracy, Andrew and Camilla, and Matt and Maxine.

There was also a surprise guest that flew in from Omaha by the name of Joe. He was the policeman near where Max lived. Myra had not told Max that he was coming.

Everyone showed up at ten in the morning. Ron was in charge of this party and was bound and determined to do the grilling but soon found himself swamped!

Max saw the problem and encouraged/pushed Willow and Ivy to help him. This solved the problem, except it did not make Peng comfortable. Willow and Ivy did not look the way they did when they were taken off the sub!

Max sat back with Joe to gaze upon the scene and talked about the past in Omaha. It appeared to them that everyone was having fun. Ivy, along with Willow was certainly enjoying helping Reverend Ron.

After awhile, Joe noticed and then informed Max that almost everyone was "packing"(carried a concealed gun). He added that Tracy's "hand cannon" was the hardest to discover, it was in her boot!

Max felt very safe after Joe's report. He figured that killers would most likely pay them a visit from Columbia someday and thought about hiring Joe for added protection. Joe had recently retired from the police force in Omaha. His work function would be billed as a security cop at the marina and church. The security room that at one time contained some of the money from the sub could be his bedroom. He could live with Fred until it was remodeled. Also, Fred could be trained by Joe to stand in for him on days he had off. Max reviewed this plan with Fred, whom agreed with it.

Max informed Joe why everyone was "packing" and then offered Joe the job to keep everyone safe while around the marina. Joe readily accepted the job. He also told Joe that this plan was reviewed with Fred and that he was looking forward to working for you.

When this information got around, everyone at the party thought it was a great idea. Towards the end of the party the adults sat together in a close circle. They all agreed that conditions were improving in the world. They also agreed that the future for their children looked better every day.

Ron was encouraged by Fred and Willow to nurse a glass of beer. After about a half hour, Ron wanted to give a talk/sermon! He started by thanking everyone for coming and then elaborated on what he felt happened in the last few years; a shadow world government, for want of a better title, created a crisis (the plague), hoping to destabilize the governments in the world. While the governments were destabilized they would attempt to implement world order under the framework of Globalism and Socialism or Communism. Of primary interest was the destruction of the government of the United States.

The henchmen in this shadow government were villains of the past who remained alive via use of the Red Pill. This pill helped double the life span of these selected people, which we now speculate included Hitler and many of his officers that fled Germany towards the end of the war. The modern day soldiers of this shadow government were the Antifa gangs and also disgruntled politicians from the period of 2016 to the present.

The finances to foot the bill was Nazi gold smuggled out of Nazi Germany and from billionaires like George Soros whom once worked for the 3rd Reich and other very rich Liberals and Globalists.

In order to accomplish this plan to overthrow the world governments, the German scientists that were taking the Red Pill, eventually developed a terrible plague, (disease), which when deployed, killed approximately half the people in the world. This was the crisis they determined would be needed to destabilize all the governments in the world. However, their plan was flawed, they did not count on people like Max that defeated their henchmen and Antifa. After Antifa was defeated in California all other states followed our example and very quickly secured their government.

To guard against this from happening again, states and federal government passed laws to outlaw shadow governments. And the people in these shadow governments would cease their activity or be prosecuted for treason!

Everyone applauded Reverend Ron's presentation. They all felt it was a good idea to incorporate the defeat of Antifa and the saving of our country in our 4th of July celebration every year.

All the adults that received a portion of the drug money from the sub were super-happy when they receive the money. They had begged Max for it and promised to keep it an utmost secret. Max was not comfortable in the arrangement but with the country in chaos, not even able to process income tax statements, he figured they were safe from the government finding out. What he worried about was the drug cartel! He would wake up at night and go over the whole sinking of the sub and grabbing the money, etc. As far as he could put things together, no one from the cartel or anyone else for that matter saw or heard anything. He told himself, that after another year goes by we should be safe!

After checking to see if the safety was off, on his 45, he joined the guests for another PBR!